...middle.

With 386 dart-holes in his head.

It had DIE, TJ, DIE written round the top in big, red letters.

It had SO LONG SCUMBAG written round the bottom in big, red letters.

Dad squeaked weirdly and went a peculiar off-white colour.

The cement-filled washing machine in my stomach switched onto SPIN.

'Is this your dartboard, Ben?' asked Mrs Block.

'No,' I said. It seemed like the only sensible answer at the time.

Breezeblock spun the dartboard round. The words b*En* Si*mP*S*on* were written across the back in my best, six-year-old handwriting.

Also available by Mark Haddon:

Agent Z Meets the Masked Crusader
Agent Z Goes Wild
Agent Z and the Penguin from Mars

For older readers:

The Curious Incident of the Dog in the Night-time

MARK HADDON

AGENT Z

and the killer bananas

RED FOX

AGENT Z AND KILLER BANANAS
A RED FOX BOOK 0 09 972481 2

First published by Red Fox, 2001
This Red Fox edition, 2005

1 3 5 7 9 10 8 6 4 2

Red Fox Books are published by Random House Children's Books,
61–63 Uxbridge Road, London W5 5SA,
a division of The Random House Group Ltd,
in Australia by Random House Australia (Pty) Ltd,
20 Alfred Street, Milsons Point, Sydney, NSW 2061, Australia,
in New Zealand by Random House New Zealand Ltd,
18 Poland Road, Glenfield, Auckland 10, New Zealand,
and in South Africa by Random House (Pty) Ltd,
Endulini, 5A Jubilee Road, Parktown 2193, South Africa

THE RANDOM HOUSE GROUP Limited Reg. No. 954009
www.kidsatrandomhouse.co.uk

A CIP catalogue record for this book is available from the British Library.

Tpyeset by Palimpsest Book Production Limited,
Polmont, Stirlingshire

Printed and bound in Great Britain by
Cox & Wyman Ltd, Reading, Berkshire

For Joe Rowland

Weetabix Volcano

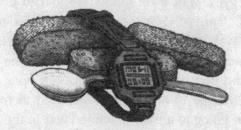

'I'll race you,' said Dad.

'You're on,' I said. I took off my watch and leant it against the HP sauce bottle in the middle of the breakfast table. I arranged three dry Weetabix in Dad's bowl and three dry Weetabix in mine.

'I'm gonna wipe the floor with you, Kiddo,' said Dad, rubbing his hands together and taking deep breaths.

'OK,' I said, 'Five. Four. Three. Two. One. GO!'

Dad stuffed two of the Weetabix into his mouth straight away and began chewing. He hadn't got the tactics sussed. Barney and I have played this game a hundred times. You just can't do three dry Weetabix in one go. You have to do them in small mouthfuls, one at a time. It's the only way.

Thirty seconds into the match and Dad was already in serious trouble. He'd run out of saliva and his jaw was beginning to seize up.

Sixty seconds into the game and the doorbell rang. Down the corridor, through the frosted glass of the front door, I could the see the postman holding a pile of mail too big to fit through the letterbox.

Dad's eyes went a bit funny. He looked over at me and said, '*Fnrgsh!*' Someone had to answer the door. Saturday was Mum's lie-in morning. If she had to get out of bed before ten she'd be homicidal. But he couldn't answer the door with his mouth locked open round a fist-sized wodge of breakfast cereal. And there was no way I was going to answer it while I was in the lead. He ran to the fridge in desperation and poured a pint of milk into his mouth. This wasn't a good tactic either because his mouth was already full of Weetabix, so the milk went over his chin and into his dressing gown.

He said, '*Fnrgsh!*' again, but louder this time and a Weetabix particle must have got lodged in his windpipe because he began choking violently.

The bell went once more. I couldn't decide whether to help Dad or go for a personal best of under two minutes. Whilst I was considering the question, the doorbell went for a third time and I heard Mum storming downstairs so it was too late anyway.

I was on my last mouthful when Mum booted the kitchen door open, threw the envelopes onto the table and said, 'Are you two *completely* . . . ?'

Then she stopped because she had just caught sight

of Dad hanging onto the corner of the freezer cabinet, his face turning purple as he tried to breathe through the impacted Weetabix.

'Trevor, what's the matter?'

'One minute fifty-seven!' I cheered as the last mouthful went down.

Dad's lungs gave one final, desperate, retching cough and the three chewed Weetabix erupted out of his mouth, spraying Mum's dressing gown with a thin layer of damp, brown flakes.

Mum thought it was quite funny. Eventually. But only after she'd had a strong coffee and a bacon sandwich. And only after Dad had mopped the floor and washed Mum's dressing gown and bought more milk and Weetabix from the corner shop. In fact she laughed so much that he decided to save his dignity by retiring to the shed for the rest of the morning.

An hour or so later I wandered down the garden with the post, which Dad had been too busy to open earlier. He was sitting at his bench doing something mechanical with the hedge-strimmer and listening to Elvis singing 'I Just Want to Be Your Teddy Bear'.

When I opened the door, he looked up and shook his head. 'Why do I let you talk me into doing these stupid things, Ben?'

'You're just easily led,' I said. I dumped the sheaf of envelopes in front of him, settled myself down on the lawnmower and took out Dr Scream's House of Horror. Dad had bought it for me the month before. He'd been changing a bulb in the lounge. He'd stuck his finger into the live socket, yelped, fallen off the stepladder and landed on Battlestar III, which Gran had given me for my birthday. He'd offered to buy me a replacement but Battlestar III was out of stock, so I'd suggested Dr Scream and by the time he realized how expensive it was he'd already promised. So he'd gritted his teeth and paid up.

Dr Scream was the business. 40 gigabytes of memory. Mini plasma screen. State of the art virtual reality interiors. And a brilliantly gruesome fantasy adventure plot.

I turned it on and loaded the half-played game I'd saved earlier. I used my bonus points to skip straight to Room 7, the kitchen, and started zapping the Slime-Monsters as they slithered out of the oven.

'What have we got here?' mumbled Dad. 'Electricity bill. Road tax reminder. *Reader's Digest* . . . And a card from my darling sister.' He read it to himself and said, 'Take a butcher's at that. Some people get all the luck.'

I hit PAUSE and took the card. On the front was a photo of a beach, palm trees, surf, the whole tropical shebang. In the background, against a ridiculously blue sky, was a big, chopped-off mountain. 'A view of the extinct Katagonga Volcano from Loopanga Beach,' said the caption. I turned it over and read the back.

Dear Trevor and Jane and Hello Ben,

Guess what? You remember Harry's great-aunt Winny? Well, she snuffed it last month. Left us three thousand smackers in the will. I'll drink to that. In fact, I am drinking to that right now. Ho ho ho. Me and

Harry are blowing the lot. *We're at the Hotel Countryclub in Talula. It's an island in the Pacific (I think). You should see it. Talk about luxury. Gold bath-taps. Gorgeous Swedish masseur. Swim-up bar in the pool. That's where I am now. On my lilo. Which is why the card's a bit soggy. OK, time to go down the shallow end for a refill, I reckon.*

Love 'n' Hugs
Trish XXXXX

I handed the card back to Dad. 'Pity that volcano's extinct.'

'Now, now,' he said, wagging a screwdriver at me. 'You may not like her very much but she *is* my sister. And these things are important.'

'I think "unfortunate" is the word you're looking for.' I unpaused Dr Scream's House of Horror and zapped a few more Slime-Monsters.

'Oh, I don't know.' Dad put his hands behind his head, leant back against the wall and stared out of the window. 'It's people like Trish and Harry who make life interesting. I mean, you can say a lot of rude things about them, but you could never accuse them of being boring.' He laughed quietly to himself. 'You remember . . .'

Dad was about to bring up the Wedding Video. It was one of his less endearing habits.

'Got to see a man about a horse,' I said. I hit PAUSE and headed for the door. 'You be careful with your fingers in those strimmer blades.'

'I don't want to be your tiger,' sang Elvis, 'Cos tigers play too rough . . .'

I headed back up the garden.

I was in need of some entertainment. But I wasn't going to get any real entertainment for at least a week. Barney was lying on a beach in Sardinia with his mum and dad. And Jenks was lying in bed with this all-over body-rash he'd picked up swimming in the canal a few days back. I was missing them badly.

There was nothing to do except wait. It was up to me and Dr Scream to entertain ourselves for the next seven days until Agent Z could swing into operation once more.

I went upstairs and lay down on my bed, exterminated the last few Slime-Monsters and headed down into the darkness of Room 8, the Cellar.

Trish and Harry Bagnell are my aunt and uncle. We see them once or twice a year at family get-togethers. Once or twice a century would be fine by me.

Harry was in the army for five years, stationed in Germany, till he got chucked out for borrowing a tank and parking it in the middle of a busy restaurant. Back in England, he set up this dodgy building firm and got married to Dad's sister. He is six foot three, plays rugby, has cauliflower ears and drinks enough beer to kill a rhinoceros. He always corners me at parties when I am trying to sneak another helping of cocktail sausages and tells me about how he bit this man's ear off in the scrum when they were playing the London Scottish C team. Then he roars with laughter and slaps me on the back and says, 'Life's not a rehearsal, Ben. You remember that. When the going gets tough, the tough get going, like we used to say in the army . . .' *Etc. Etc. Etc.*

Trish is worse. She has peroxide blonde hair, five-inch heels and low-cut dresses that show off her pumpkin-sized bosoms. She chain-smokes menthol cigarettes and drinks triple gins until she can't cope with the five-inch heels any more. Then she twists her ankle and starts shouting at people and Harry has to take her home.

She used to come up to me when I was talking to Mum and start pawing my biceps and say, 'He's going to grow up into something extremely tasty, I'll tell you that for nothing, Jane.' Then she'd cackle like a witch, breathe smoke in my face and smooch day-glo pink lipstick all over my cheek.

The Bagnells have two kids. Charlene is twenty-five and lives in Doncaster with a nightclub manager called Des. TJ is sixteen and a liability. Ever since I was tiny, I can remember hearing stories of his latest exploits. How he'd set light to the sofa with a box of matches. How he'd sellotaped his gerbil to a model plane and flown it across the dual carriageway. How he'd broken his leg trying to put a friend's underpants on the top of the flag-pole at his dad's rugby club. But it wasn't until Charlene's wedding that I realized he was the Son of Satan.

I was sitting round the back of the marquee towards the end of the reception, feeling bored and waiting to go home, when TJ came up to me and started boasting about his pet tarantula. I asked him why he was drinking chocolate milkshake and he laughed and said it wasn't chocolate milkshake. He asked if I wanted to try some and I said, 'OK.'

'Like it?' he asked.

'Yeah,' I said.

So he wandered off and got me a pint of the stuff. What he didn't tell me was that it was a Brandy Alexander, the biggest Brandy Alexander in the History of Western Civilization. This was two years ago and I wasn't very clued up about alcohol at the time. I thought it all tasted revolting, like Dad's Guinness. This stuff, however, tasted *fantastic*.

I drank half of it straight off. After a few minutes I looked at TJ and started feeling really friendly towards him and decided that maybe I'd got him all wrong and he was quite a nice person after all. Except I couldn't work out why he was talking nonsense. Or why the garden seemed to be lurching from side to side. A couple of minutes later, everything went blank. The next thing I remember was opening my eyes and seeing Mum perched on the edge of my bed holding a bucket, and this pain in my head like someone had hit me with a cricket bat.

A month later we were invited to the Bagnells' to watch the first screening of the wedding video. We'd almost reached the end when TJ said, 'Hang on. This is the best bit.'

Suddenly TJ's grinning face appeared on the screen in gruesome close-up. He winked and turned the camera round and began carrying it out of the marquee on to the lawn. The awful truth began to dawn. The camera tracked round to the back of the marquee and there I was, up on the screen, in front of everyone, with Charlene's posy on my head, waving my arms in the air, singing, 'Look at me! I'm a tree!'

I sat frozen with horror as the video camera followed me across the lawn and into the house. I staggered into the hall, tripped on the mat and clung to the banisters, saying, 'Everything's wobbly, TJ. All wobbly. Wobbly and nobbly.'

I stumbled slowly up the stairs. At the top of the stairs my legs gave way and I began crawling along the landing carpet, saying, 'I'm not a tree now. I'm a lizard.' And then, 'Where's the loo, TJ?'

I dragged myself to my feet and staggered into the nearest bedroom. TJ got the camera round the door just in time to see me opening a cupboard, sticking my head inside and throwing up.

Then the screen went blank.

And Trish stopped laughing like a drain. She turned round in her seat and gave me the Look of Death and said, 'So *that's* what happened to my fur coat!'

There were three seconds of uncomfortable silence then the riot started. Mum suddenly realized that I didn't get gastro-enteritis from the smoked salmon after all. Trish wanted me to cough up fifty pounds for the dry-cleaning. And I wanted to strangle TJ.

For a few minutes, it looked as if someone was going to end up in Casualty. Then Dad dragged me and Mum out to the car and we drove away like we were leaving a bank raid.

Understandably the Bagnells are not my favourite topic of conversation.

I didn't give them another thought until the following evening.

I was sitting on the sofa at the time, finishing my rum baba and cutting my toenails. Mum was admiring the drawings of nude men she'd done at her life drawing class. Badger, our Very Very Old English Sheep Dog, was gumming a slipper to death. And Dad was watching the news.

'I think I should do some sketches of you, Trevor,' said Mum dreamily. 'So I can show my handsome husband off to everyone else in the art class.'

'*Gordon Bennett!*' said Dad.

'Don't worry. You could keep your undies on,' added Mum.

But Dad wasn't talking about posing nude. 'I think you must be psychic, Ben,' he said. 'Look.'

I glanced up at the television.

'Katagonga last erupted in 1867,' said the newsreader, 'and was thought to be extinct. A team of geologists were preparing to fly to the island yesterday when the volcano erupted. According to eye-witness reports there is now a river of molten lava flowing across the island and into the harbour.

'Earlier today, I spoke to Hamish MacLister, a Scotsman who farms kiwi fruit on the island.'

The newsreader disappeared and was replaced by a map of the Pacific Ocean. Halfway between Papua New

Guinea and South America was the word TALULA and an arrow pointing to a gnat-dropping circled in red.

'We thought it was the end of the world, mate,' said a voice so crackly it sounded as if the man was walking through cornflakes. 'There was this bloody great bang and then the sky went dark.'

'And what does the scene look like now?' asked the newsreader.

'Well, if I look out the window I can see . . . My sainted . . . ! Sheila! Grab the dog! I'll get the car keys! *Now! Move it!*'

The phone went dead and the newsreader reappeared. 'Travel companies report that a number of British tourists are on Talula at present, though we have not managed to confirm their safety or whereabouts.'

Dad pressed the MUTE button on the TV zapper and flopped backwards into the sofa.

'I hope they remembered to take their asbestos swimming trunks,' I said, and it seemed really funny when I said it. And then it didn't seem so funny because Mum glared at me and said, 'Ben, that is *sick*,' and I realized that Trish and Harry and TJ might actually be dead.

I nudged Badger. 'Come on, Doggins. Time for walkies, I think.'

Return of the Brandy Alexander Monster

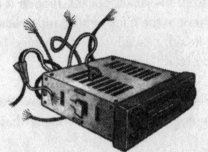

I was sitting on the bench outside the Seven-Eleven eating a bag of chips and onion rings when the smoked-glass Cadillac pulled up. It idled at the kerb with the engine purring for several seconds, then the driver's door opened. A body-builder in wrap-around shades and a tight white T-shirt climbed out and opened the back passenger door. A distinguished, elderly man in a very expensive black suit stepped onto the pavement using a carved walking stick with a handle shaped like a monkey's head. The muscled flunky closed the car door behind him and the two men walked over to the bench.

The older man eyed me up and down before saying, 'So you're Ben Simpson, the guy who predicted the Katagonga eruption.'

'Yep,' I replied, chewing an onion ring. 'And you're Lorenzo Giordano.'

The man's eyes widened. He turned to his driver and said, 'Hey, this kid's good.'

'Casino owner and gun-runner . . .' I continued.

'Keep it down, Wise-Guy,' he said. 'We don't want the place swarming with cops.' He sat himself on the bench, took a coin from his jacket pocket, flipped it into the air and slapped it onto the back of his hand. 'Heads or tails?'

'Neither,' I said, casually. 'It's a Chicago bus token.'

'So . . . you really are psychic.'

'Yup.'

An evil grin cracked his wrinkled face. 'You and me, boy, we're going to make more money than you ever dreamed of.'

'The Central Reserve Bank of Chicago, right? And you want me to give you the code to the main vault.'

'The kid's a genius.'

'No way, *José*.'

'All I need is a number. You sit at home and twiddle your thumbs and three weeks from now I open a Swiss bank account in your name with fifty big ones in it.'

'Sadly not,' I replied. 'Three weeks from now you're going to be lying in the Beth Israel Medical Centre while they dig out the bullets pumped into your butt by Joey Chan during the shoot-out in Dino's Clothing Warehouse.'

Lorenzo narrowed his eyes and started at me. 'Are you stringing me a line, Kid?'

I shrugged. 'Who's the psychic here, me or you?'

His face went white and his hands began to shake.

He got up slowly from the bench and said, 'Are you going to eat this bread pudding or not?'

Then he started going all fuzzy and the Cadillac disappeared and I realized that I was staring at the plastic Messerchmitt mobile dangling from my bedroom ceiling.

'Ben!' shouted Mum from downstairs. 'It's been sitting here for ten minutes. Are you going to come and eat it or not?'

I was daydreaming again. It's a hobby of mine. Some kids keep hamsters. Some do gymnastics, or set fire to sofas. Me, I daydream. A lot. Especially during the school holidays. Especially when Barney's sunning himself in the Med and Jenks is suffering from the Black Death.

Dad says it's a complete waste of time. But his hobby is Elvis Presley so he hasn't got a leg to stand on, frankly. Mum says it's because I'm a sensitive young man with a creative mind. I tend to agree with Mum on this one.

'Ben!!!'

'Coming!' I levered myself off the bed, rubbed my eyes and headed down towards the kitchen.

I dolloped a serving of bread pudding into a bowl and sauntered through to the lounge. Mum was doing a charcoal drawing of Badger and watching *Dalston Junction*. I plonked myself down beside her.

'What do you think?' she asked, showing me the picture.

'Doesn't look anything like Dad,' I said.

'You watch it, you cheeky monkey,' she said, and

whacked me round the head with her sketchpad. 'Now shut up,' she said. 'This bit's important.'

On screen, there was a ruckus at the Aquarius Hair Salon.

'There's nothing wrong with my Darren,' growled Pam from under her hair dryer.

'Apart from having forty-three tattoos,' replied Doreen from under the adjacent dryer. 'And the IQ of plywood.'

'You cow!' spat Pam, grabbing a pair of hot curling tongs and lunging towards Doreen as the scene flipped to the toilets of the Blue Lagoon Bar 'n' Grill where Benny was trying on the new toupee he had bought after the accident with the blowtorch.

And then the phone rang. The real phone. In our house. Not in *Dalston Junction*.

Mum headed off to the hall and I flicked channels and watched three minutes of a documentary about a man whose leg was eaten by piranha fish. Then Mum reappeared. I flicked back to *Dalston Junction*.

'Well,' she said, picking up her sketchpad and sitting down, 'Trish and Harry are alive.'

'So, what's the news?'

Mum shook her head and laughed. 'She was ringing from the hotel bar. Strangely enough. She said they'd been really lucky because the wind was in the right direction so the volcano kind of went the other way.'

On screen, Pam and Terry were having their late-night cocoa when Darren swaggered in and dropped his Spurs bag on the floor. The bag fell open and a battered car stereo rolled out.

16

Terry picked up the stereo and examined it. 'This is *ours.*'

'Is it?' said Darren. 'Sorry, Dad. It was bit dark, see. Being at night and stuff.'

'You gormless prat!' shouted Pam. 'You're meant to nick stuff from *other people.*'

'Unfortunately,' continued Mum, turning back to me, 'the airport doesn't exist any more, so they're kind of stuck there.'

'What a terrible position for them to be in,' I said, tutting and wiping my bowl with a breadcrust.

'I don't think it's bothering them overmuch. The holiday insurance will pay for them to stay at the hotel till they're rescued. Bar bill included. So they're having a whale of a time. As you can imagine.'

'What about Total Jerk?'

'Well, that's the weird thing,' said Mum. 'Trish was just saying what a laugh it was, and how Harry was having caviar on his cornflakes seeing as someone else was paying. Then she said, "But I have to tell you about TJ . . ."'

'Yeah?'

'And the phone went dead.'

'She was probably wiped out by a stream of lava coursing through the hotel bar,' I said. 'And she'll be buried for thousands of years and they'll dig her up like those people from Pompeii and put her in a glass box in a museum and she'll be standing there, all brown and crusty, talking into a fossilized phone, with a menthol cigarette in one hand and a gin in the other . . .'

'I never cease to be amazed by how generous and

warm-hearted you are, Ben,' said Mum, returning to the portrait of Badger and taking special care over the difficult bits where his leg-hair has fallen off in clumps due to his eczema.

A couple of days later I was lounging on the sofa watching *Revenge of the Swamp Thing* and eating the last of my homemade chicken-soup lollies when I was vaguely aware of a knock at the door. The Swamp Thing had just swum up a sewer and found its way into an unsuspecting vicar's bathroom when Mum opened the lounge door behind me.

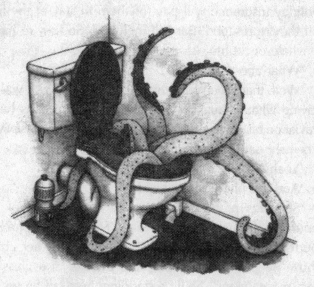

'Well,' she said, 'now we know what happened to TJ.'
'I guess fried alive is too much to hope for.'
There was an odd silence, so I turned round. TJ was

standing in the doorway holding a rucksack and giving me a Wait-Till-the-Two-of-Us-Are-Alone kind of smile.

'What's *he* doing here?' I asked. It didn't seem worth being diplomatic, seeing as I'd already blown that one.

'I was on a camping holiday with this mate, Garry, and his folks,' said TJ. 'Came back to the house and no one was in. Then I heard about this volcano thing. Reckoned I might be able to kip down here for a few days till the folks get back.'

A look of profound horror passed across Mum's face.

'Why can't you stay with Garry?' I asked.

'Yes,' agreed Mum, perking up, 'that sounds like a jolly good idea.'

'I'm not exactly in their good books at the moment. Like, they were asleep in their tent and we tied their guy-rope to a cow and . . .'

'Neighbours?' asked Mum, in one last desperate attempt to save us all.

'I knocked on their door. But they wouldn't answer. And, anyway, what's the big deal here? It's not like I'm asking much. And you're *family*, right?'

Mum looked at me and winced. 'You'll have to share Ben's room, I'm afraid . . .'

I turned back to *Revenge of the Swamp Thing*. 'Fine,' I said, 'I'll move into the shed.'

Sled-Ride to the Lair of the
Vampire Afghan

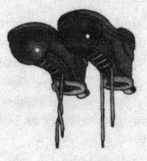

'We have no choice,' said Major Ölafson. 'We have to turn back.'

'I'm taking those huskies to the Pole,' I replied. 'I didn't come all this way for nothing.'

The wind wailed viciously outside the snowhole.

'You're crazy,' he said, shaking his head. 'It's minus seventy out there. It's a total white-out. Your leg's gangrenous and we've lost radio contact.'

'So, I'm crazy. If I wasn't crazy I wouldn't be here in the first place. I'm going. Period. You can come with me or you can stay here.'

'We'll die,' he said grimly.

'True. But we'll die anyway. We've got three tins of

beans, a Kendal Mint Cake and half a sachet of milk powder. That's not going to get us back to McMurdo Sound. We've got a week to live, at most. We can spend it trying to get to the pole. Or we can spend it running away. It's as simple as that, Sven. And I know how *I* want to be remembered.'

Suddenly, a ghostly figure appeared in the doorway of the snowhole carrying a mug of hot chocolate and a bowl of Shreddies.

'Oh, hi, Mum,' I said.

She closed the shed door behind her, perched on the lawnmower and handed me my breakfast.

'Room service. Cheers. You're a quality parent.'

'Ben,' she said, 'honestly. This is ridiculous. You know I'm not one for playing the heavy-handed mother, but I do think you're being a bit childish.'

'That's because I'm a child.'

'You're never going to get on with TJ if you spend your whole time avoiding him.'

'I'm never going to get on with TJ. Ever. So, avoiding him seems like a pretty good plan from where I'm sitting.'

'Well, it doesn't make me feel very good having to apologize for your bizarre behaviour.'

'*You're* apologizing to *him*?'

'It's called being diplomatic, Ben. It's part of being a grown-up.'

'And I suppose you're having a great time sharing the house with him, aren't you?'

She raised an eyebrow at me. 'No, actually. It's a living nightmare. It's called Putting Up With Your Husband's

21

Family And Not Complaining. Which is another part of being a grown-up. But that's not why I came down here . . . Barney rang. They got back from Sardinia last night. And Jenks' rash has cleared up, apparently. He wants you to meet him at the Command Centre, wherever *that* happens to be.'

'Sorry. Classified information,' I replied, feeling almost cheerful. I got out of my sleeping bag and stood up. 'I'll catch you later, OK?'

'What about your chocolate and Shreddies?' she asked.

'Oh yeah. Thanks.' I grabbed them and headed for the door. 'Breakfast on the hoof again. It's all go for the modern kid.'

'You stay out of trouble,' she said.

I paused on the threshold and turned round. She looked a bit emotional, the way she does when people are kissing in black and white films on the telly. 'Are you all right?' I asked.

She sighed and raised one eyebrow microscopically. 'I wish *I* had a shed to move into.'

I walked back over to the lawnmower and patted her shoulder. 'It's all yours. Get into the sleeping bag, put some Elvis on the ghetto blaster and help yourself to the Mars Bars behind the potting compost. If I bump into Total Jerk I'll tell him you went into town to have your perm resprayed.'

Mum smiled and ruffled my hair. 'I'm sorely tempted, Ben. Sorely tempted.'

'See you later.' I pecked her on the cheek, left the shed and headed up the garden, spooning Shreddies into my mouth and slopping hot chocolate all over the crazy paving.

Being grown-up had been particularly difficult for Mum and Dad over the past twelve hours. After our icy introduction, TJ had marched upstairs to my room, emptied his rucksack onto the floor and suspended my old teddy bear from the curtain rail with a hangman's noose made out of one of my school ties. He'd changed into a T-shirt with the words I'M SO PERFECT on the front and sprayed his armpits with eight litres of *Homme Sauvage* anti-perspirant.

He'd then gone downstairs and made himself an industrial-size cheese and pickle sandwich with all the remaining Wensleydale, then sloped out onto the drive where Dad was under the bonnet of the Escort. TJ had stood behind him for fifteen minutes saying things like, 'You're not meant to do it that way, Trevor,' and staring at girls walking down the street and shouting, 'Babe-Alert! Babe-Alert!'

Eventually, Dad had said very quietly, 'Please go away, TJ, or I am going to kill you.'

'You're a tough man, Uncle Trev,' TJ had laughed, slapping Dad on the back and making him bang his head on the bonnet.

At lunch, he'd asked Mum if she'd put on a bit of weight. When Dad said he was off to one of his Rock 'n' Roll nights, TJ had laughed out loud, assuming it was some kind of joke. And when he'd finally finished eating, he'd pushed his chair back, said, 'Top tucker, Mrs S,'

23

and let out a belch loud enough to break a window.

I remember glancing down at Dad's fingers tightening round the handle of the carving knife and hoping that Harry and Trish got back before my parents ended up in prison.

I took my new mountain bike from its parking spot down the side of the house. I grabbed my D-lock, tied Badger's lead to the end of the handlebars and headed down to the park. We skirted the boating lake and ducked through the hole in the fence onto the wasteground. I locked the bike up, removed Badger's lead and told him I'd be back in half an hour. I commando-crawled through the grass towards the rusty yellow bulldozer, waited until the coast was clear then sprinted over the open ground towards the back of the old park-keeper's cottage.

I levered up the stray board from the cellar window and slipped into the concrete chute. I replaced the board, squirmed through the window, jumped down onto the cellar floor and made my way to the stairs. The house was oddly silent. I went up to the ground floor, walked along the hallway, saw no light coming from under the door to the Command Centre and pushed it open.

Pitch darkness.

Something was wrong.

I stepped forward gingerly.

There was a click and, suddenly, a torchlight went on. I yelped. Six inches in front of me was Jenks' face. Suspended. Upside down. In mid-air. Wearing luminous green vampire-fangs.

'Welcome to the Bat Cavern, puny mortal!' he said.

'Holy Cow!' I gasped, breathing deeply.

'Good, eh?' said Barney, flicking back the mildewed curtains and letting the daylight back into the room. 'Found an old pair of walking boots in the attic at home. Borrowed Dad's drill and bolted them to the ceiling. Bit tricky getting up there but I reckon the effect's worth it.'

'What we really need is a coffin,' said Jenks, 'but you don't get many coffins in skips.'

Barney, Jenks and I are the Crane Grove Crew.

Barney is the kind of kid your parents like. He always has seconds when he comes round for tea. He says things like, 'That new avocado bathroom suite is rather nice, Mrs Simpson,' or, 'I see you went for the JVC 467D stack system with the quad speakers, Mr Jenkinson.' He has grown-ups wrapped round his little finger.

What grown-ups don't realize is that he is just as good at gluing someone's trousers to the chair during Biology, or dropping plastic centipedes into the refrigerated deli counter at Sainsburys. He has the brain of a nuclear physicist and the body of someone who has been having second helpings for a very long time indeed.

Jenks, on the other hand, is the kind of kid parents do their best to keep out of their houses altogether. He is guaranteed to spill hot chocolate into the back of the JVC 467D stack system, or bring down the shower-curtain doing gibbon impressions.

He has the mind of a sea-urchin and the body of a pencil on account of the fact that he's never finished a first helping in his life. He simply doesn't sit still long enough. There are at least seven kids in his family. I'm never sure of the exact number. None of them sit still long enough to be counted. They are all hyperactive.

Earlier this summer they were having coffee at a motorway service station on the M42 when Jenks' little brother, Wayne, decided to explore the back of a nearby dumper truck. No one knew where he was until the driver decided to check on his cargo of sand just north of Dundee. A couple of weeks back his younger sister, Brenda, had to be taken to Casualty after she climbed into one of the machines at the laundrette and did 6 minutes on the WOOLLENS cycle for a bet. And it wasn't just the kids. Jenks' dad is the only man in the building industry to have accidentally demolished an entire house while putting a doorbell in, after driving a nail through the gas main.

Life is pretty dull round our way, unless you get a thrill out of Turtle-Waxing the Nissan Micra and buying hardy perennials from the garden centre. Like Dad says, you have to have Something-to-Stop-You-Going-Completely-Mad. For him it's Elvis. For Mum it's *Dalston Junction* and drawing naked men. For Barney, Jenks and me it's practical jokes.

Like gluing up the nozzles of the plastic ketchup bottles at school, then making a tiny hole in the bottom, so that people turn them upside down and squeeze extra hard to get some ketchup out and send pints of the stuff rocketing towards the ceiling.

Or like fooling our next-door neighbour into thinking

26

he's been visited by alien beings, which we did last summer, using nothing more than a borrowed penguin, a roll of Bacofoil and a slice of purple meteorite from Sandy Creek, Wyoming.

You get the picture.

We run the operation from the lounge of the derelict park-keeper's cottage on the wasteground next to the park and work under the code-name 'Agent Z'. We swear oaths of secrecy and promise to die before betraying the Agent Z Code of Honour.

I stepped round Jenks and threw myself down onto the tattered sofa. 'God, am I glad to see you two.'

'I can understand that,' said Barney. 'Life without us must be sheer hell.' He opened the door of the ancient, non-functioning fridge and took out three cans of Tango. He threw one to Jenks and one to me. 'But we're back now, so you can breathe easy again.'

'Not exactly,' I said, glumly.

He came over and sat down and slipped into his caring American therapist voice. 'Tell me about it, Ben. I think you'll find it helps to talk.'

'Remember that volcano?' I asked. 'The one that erupted last week?' Out of the corner of my eye, I could see Jenks trying to open a can of Tango while suspended from the ceiling by his feet.

'Uh-huh.'

'My aunt and uncle were on the island.'

'Mad Aunt Gwen and the Blubber Mountain?'

'No. Dad's sister and her husband. Trish and Harry.'

'Oh, the Beer-Sponge and Mrs Cleavage. They dead, then?'

'No. But they're stuck out there because the airport's covered in lava. Except TJ was camping in the Lake District with a friend. And now he's staying with us.'

'Ouch.'

'In *my* room.'

I glanced over my shoulder and saw that Jenks had finally got the tab off the can and was gingerly starting to sip at it.

'Hang on a mo,' said Barney. 'I've got to record this for posterity.'

He leant over the arm of the chair, picked up a brand new camcorder, hoicked it smoothly to his shoulder and switched it on. I heard a muffled choke and turned to see Jenks bucking and twisting in his vampire boots, squeezing his nose between his fingers and going blue in the face. Drinking Tango upside down was clearly harder than it looked.

'Lights! Camera! Action!' said Barney.

Jenks couldn't hold out any longer. He released his nose and let out a huge, hacking cough. Two high-pressure fountains of Tango and snot erupted from his nostrils, narrowly missing the arm of the sofa. He doubled up and coughed again. The roof-beam couldn't take it any longer. There was a big, crunchy rip from above our heads and the circle of plaster round the vampire boots tore itself loose.

'Whoo-ergh!' gurgled Jenks through a pint of fizzing orange phlegm, and plummeted to the ground, jamming his head into the opening of his Adidas bag.

'Another comedy classic in the can,' said Barney, pressing the STOP button and turning to me. 'Good, isn't it? I won it in this competition on the back of a Bran Flakes packet. Dad's friend Clive works for the ad agency. He said he'd jot down the right answers for me if I promised to give him a bottle of Jim Beam whiskey at Christmas. It's digital, too. So you can edit the videos on a computer and add effects and stuff.' He leant forward. 'You all right down there, Jenks?'

'I think so,' winced Jenks, rubbing his bruised head and wiping the bubbly sludge from his face.

Barney turned back to me. 'I suppose doing something nasty to TJ's out of the question, what with him being a member of your family *and* a psychopath.'

'Fraid so,' I said. 'I'm just going to have to put up with him until they de-lava the airport.'

'In which case,' said Barney, 'we should do our best to take your mind off the whole ghastly situation.' He stood up, dumped the video camera in Jenks' Adidas bag, then looped it over his shoulder.

'Oi!' said Jenks. 'Where are you going with that?'

'*We*,' replied Barney, 'are going to the Grosvenor Centre.'

'Why?' I asked.

Barney fished around in his jacket pocket, pulled out a fiver and handed it to me. The Queen had a large biro moustache and was wearing a bright red Z badge on her lapel. I was just turning the note over to see what Barney had done on the back when the note leapt out of my hands.

'Wha . . . ?'

'Fishing twine,' explained Barney, dangling the note in front of me, then repocketing it.

'I don't understand,' said Jenks.

Barney tapped the side of his nose. 'Follow me.'

Fifteen minutes later we were sitting in the Friary café in the main aisle of the Grosvenor Centre. I was drinking a Pepsi float. Jenks was standing beside a large potted palm tree outside Boots with his foot on the fiver. And Barney was sipping black coffee, twiddling the knobs on the concealed camera and adjusting his grip on the fishing twine beneath the table.

'OK,' said Barney, after a few minutes, 'Jenks . . . ?'

Jenks took his foot off the fiver, walked over and sat down on the far side of the table. Barney hit PLAY.

Nine people walked past the fiver without noticing it. A toddler on baby-reins noticed it, bent down to pick it up and was hauled away as its mother carried on striding towards WHSmith's. Another six people walked past the fiver until, finally, a shaven-headed builder in paint-splattered jeans stooped to pick it up and was rather taken aback when it slithered away from him. He stooped again. It slithered again. He realized something fishy was going on, pretended to be retying his shoelaces, then vanished into the crowd.

Jenks headed off to the counter to get supplies.

An elderly nun looked at it, dithered, then decided against picking it up. A man in an Aston Villa T-shirt did a goalie-dive to catch the fiver and hurt his shoulder quite badly on the potted palm tree. Two kids went for it simultaneously, banged heads, started fighting and had to be separated by a security guard.

'It's *quite* funny,' said Barney, as the camcorder hummed quietly in Jenks' bag. 'But it's not *brilliantly* funny, is it? You see, I've been thinking. What I reckon we should do is . . .'

'Here you are,' said Jenks, returning from the counter with three almond slices and 6p's worth of change.

'Cheers,' said Barney, launching into the first almond slice. 'What we should do is use the camcorder to make a *real* film. None of this cheapskate *You've Been Framed* rubbish. The genuine article. Spies. Car-chases. Fights. Stunts. The works.'

'Yeah,' said Jenks, jiggling in his seat. 'And we could have, like, these really terrifying hundred-foot tyrannosauruses which come out of this time-tunnel thing and stamp all over people's houses and eat everyone alive and they have to attack them with helicopter gunships and . . .'

Barney patted him on the arm. 'Let's start with the easy stuff, eh?'

My mind was whizzing. 'It could be a ghost story,' I said.

Barney ummed and erred. 'Possibly. But ghost stories usually happen at night, right? So the lighting would be tricky.'

'OK, then,' I suggested. 'A thriller. And we could have special effects. Like when a building blows up, but it's actually just a model. Or when someone gets shot,

31

except it's just a bag of fake blood bursting under their shirt . . .'

'You're getting the hang of it,' said Barney, starting on the second almond slice.

For the first time in four days, I had completely forgotten about TJ.

Unfortunately we had also forgotten about the fishing twine and the fiver. This wouldn't have mattered were it not for one small piece of extremely bad luck.

It was Jenks who noticed it first. Barney and I saw his jaw drop and turned round to see what he was staring at.

On the far side of the aisle, beside the potted palm, stood Mrs Block, our headmistress. She was holding a large bag of shopping in one hand and the fiver in the other, narrowing her eyes as she examined the Queen's moustache and Z badge.

At this precise moment a large Afghan hound and its owner passed between us and Breezeblock. The Afghan caught its paw in the twine and tripped. As it stumbled, a second paw became tangled. It panicked and bolted. The twine must have been wound round Breezeblock somehow because a fraction of a second later she was yanked off her feet, hurling her bag of shopping high into the air above her head.

Time seemed to slow down. I watched a jar of Branston pickle and a box of All Bran revolve gracefully in the air before turning earthwards. Then the pandemonium began. Two sherry bottles exploded on the tiled floor. The Branston pickle landed, someone shouted, 'It's a bomb!' and the Afghan began baying like a wolf.

We watched in frozen horror as Breezeblock got to her knees and began reeling in the twine, yelling, 'I've got the culprits!' like a very angry fisherman who has just caught a very big fish.

The line went tight in Barney's hand and we were about four nanoseconds away from being discovered when the owner of the Afghan hound lost his footing in the slurry of yoghurt, sherry and All Bran, skidded and fell over, taking the headmistress with him just before she caught sight of us in the Friary café.

Barney turned to Jenks and me. 'Time for us to go, I think.'

We went.

Fast.

Blackmail

We headed over to Barney's place and played the video of *Breezeblock Comes a Cropper* forty-seven times. Sure, it was excellent entertainment watching our headmistress turning somersaults but, to be honest, it sent a chill down my spine every time I saw her scrutinizing that five-pound note with its incriminating Z badge on the royal lapel. But, hey, as Barney said, how could she possibly connect that with us?

Afterwards I cycled home for lunch, opened the front door and was greeted by the roar of ten thousand Blackburn Rovers fans singing, 'Here we go! Here we go! Here we go!' from the television in the lounge. I dropped my bag by the telephone table and walked down the hall to the kitchen. TJ stood up from the biscuit cupboard with a stack of seven chocolate Hob-Nobs in his hand.

'Wotcha, Small Fry!' he said, frisbeeing one of the Hob-Nobs into the air and positioning himself underneath it so that it came down directly into his cavernous gob.

'Where are Mum and Dad?' I asked.

'Ran away,' he said. 'Couldn't stand you any longer. Leapt into a taxi about half an hour ago.' He looked at me and winked. 'Actually, your dad's down the bottom of the garden in your new bedroom, listening to that prehistoric Elvis garbage and your mum's upstairs. And if you're looking for your lunch, I've eaten it.'

I glared at him and visualized someone driving a fence-post through the top of his head with a sledgehammer.

'Loosen up, Cuz.' He squidged my cheek between his thumb and forefinger and laughed. 'Only having a chuckle. It's in the microwave.'

I waited till he'd returned to the TV, then heated my mushroom soup for two minutes on MAX, added ketchup, grabbed a slice of bread and headed for the stairs.

'On the other hand,' shouted TJ from the lounge, 'I *did* blow my nose in it.'

Mum was lying on her bed doing a bathroom-object still-life in charcoal – a rucked-up flannel, a can of athlete's foot-spray, a wind-up frog and the pink shower-cap that Mad Aunt Gwen had left behind when she last stayed over.

I sat down on the bed, decided that TJ was probably just winding me up about the soup and risked a mouthful.

35

'You hiding?' I asked.

'Yup,' said Mum.

The soup tasted fine. 'Is that part of being grown-up, too?'

'Nope.'

I tutted. 'You know I'm not the one to play the heavy-handed son but I do think you're being a bit childish.'

'OK, point taken,' she said. 'Everything still all right down there? He hasn't set light to the sofa, or rung Nigeria and left the phone off the hook?'

'Well, the sofa's still in one piece, anyway.'

'Honestly,' Mum huffed, dropping her pad and her stick of charcoal onto the bedroom floor. 'He puts his muddy feet up on the coffee table. He orders me to rustle up sandwiches like I'm some serving wench. He listens to tuneless screeching music till three in the morning. He bangs doors. He leaves globs of toothpaste round the sink. And he actually thinks he's *funny*. This morning I get a film back from the chemist and what's the last photo of? Your moronic cousin holding the camera at arm's length and grinning into the lens with two tomato-halves over his eyes and a slice of melon jammed into his mouth.' She glanced at her watch. 'Crikey!'

'What?'

'*Dalston Junction*! Omnibus edition!'

Mum leapt off the bed, dropping her sketchbook behind her and exiting the room at high speed. The mattress boinged and the remains of the mushroom soup flipped out of the bowl onto the charcoal still-life. I tried to wipe it with my sleeve. This didn't help. I hid the sketchbook under the mattress and followed Mum downstairs, carrying the empty bowl.

By the time I reached the lounge the argument was already in full flow.

'Aw! Come on. It's the quarter final. And it's Blackburn, too. And you've already seen both episodes of *Dalston Junction* this week. Fair's fair.'

'I'm not talking *fair*, TJ. I'm talking *my* television.'

'I mean, it's only a rubbishy soap . . .'

'TJ, I am warning you . . .'

I went through to the kitchen, dropped the soup-bowl in the sink and headed down the garden.

Dad was seated at his workbench doing something fiddly to the insides of a small pink gadget.

'What's that?' I asked, settling myself down on the sleeping bag and retrieving Dr Scream's House of Horror from my jacket pocket.

'Mum's Ladyshave,' said Dad.

'Yuck,' I said. I used my bonus to skip straight to the Cellar, zapped the two torches on the wall to set them alight so that I could see what I was doing, zapped open the cover of the big, leather book, then zapped the Pentangle in the middle of the open page.

The screen began to shimmer.

'My shaver was on the blink this morning,' said Dad. 'Decided to borrow your mother's. Blew up halfway through a sideburn. There was a loud clanking noise then this explosion as it dug itself into my cheek.' He turned to show me the large, bloodstained Elastoplast where his right sideburn used to be. 'I don't think I've felt anything

37

quite so painful since I hammered my finger to the tree putting that blasted birdhouse up.' He poked around in the intestines of the shaver with his needle-nosed pliers. 'So either I fix it, or I cough up forty quid for a new one.'

While I was dematerializing and waiting to re-materialize in the Torture Attic I fished around behind the bag of compost with my free hand. 'Hey. My Mars Bars have gone.'

'Yeah. Sorry about that,' said Dad.

'There were five of them,' I replied.

'I was a bit peckish.' Dad shrugged in self-defence. He put down the pliers, picked up a couple of screws and began slotting them back into their holes. 'I'll buy you some more tomorrow. Promise.'

'But there's nine hundredweight of macaroni cheese in the fridge . . .'

'I know. I know.'

'Are you doing a Mum?' I hit PAUSE.

'What's "Doing a Mum"?'

'Avoiding TJ.'

'That sounds about right.' He put down the screw-driver and picked up the back of the shaver-cover.

'I don't know . . .' I sighed. 'You're a couple of Wendies, you two.'

'I'll be honest with you, Ben,' Dad said, squeezing the two halves of the shaver together. 'And this is not a nice thing to say, but I only have to look at that boy and I feel ill.'

'Sounds perfectly normal to me,' I said.

'It gets worse,' Dad continued. 'Trish rang again today.

The airport's not going to be sorted out till 2030, so they'll have to be picked up by boat. And since Talula's several thousand miles from the rest of civilization they're not going to be back for another month at least.' The two halves of the shaver did not want to go back together again. Dad squeezed harder. 'So, we are going to have to make some arrangement for him to go to school.'

The shaver erupted in Dad's hands. 457 tiny, separate electrical components sprang into the air and fell like lumpy rain inside the shed.

'*Your* school.'

My school.

For the last few days I'd been consoling myself with the thought that school would be an escape. The Napoleonic wars, electrons, Pythagoras, the sex life of the earthworm . . . and no TJ. Bliss. Now we would never be more than two hundred metres away from each other until his parents came to retrieve him.

Dad stared at the 457 tiny, separate electrical components littering the shed floor, then leant forward and banged his head against the edge of the workbench fifteen or twenty times, moaning quietly to himself.

I unpaused Dr Scream. The Torture Attic materialized in front of me. In the centre of the darkened room, a man was bolted down to a table. A large circular saw whizzed between his legs, slicing through the table and rapidly approaching his important bits. 'Save me! Save me!' said a squeaky voice from the microspeaker. A clock in the corner of the screen was ticking away. Ten seconds. Nine seconds . . . I looked around for something to zap.

I zapped the hunchbacked saw-operator with the twisty yellow teeth. I zapped the circular saw itself. I zapped the cuffs. I zapped everything. I was too late. One second. Zero. The saw reached the victim's doodahs, and the screen was splattered in blood which dripped slowly away to reveal the words DR SCREAM WINS AGAIN . . . COME BACK SOON FOR MORE . . . IF YOU DARE.

Halfway through the afternoon, I decided to retrieve a few things from my room. I opened the door without knocking, to emphasize the point that this was *my* room, and marched in.

A cassette of guitar-thrash noise was playing on my ghetto blaster and TJ was sitting on the sill of the open window, sucking on a cigarette and blowing the smoke out across the front garden.

I took three pairs of underpants and one pair of socks from the chest of drawers. I picked up my Swiss army knife, my cap-gun, my Boston Red Sox baseball cap and my copy of *The Loch Ness Monster: Fact or Fiction?* I grabbed my ghetto-blaster, hit STOP, ejected the tape, unplugged it, grabbed the handle and headed towards the door.

'What is it with you lot?' sneered TJ.

I turned and looked at him. For one brief moment I imagined running across the room and shoving him out of the window. It was a tempting idea. Except, of course, that TJ would then be dead and I'd end up in some special high security hospital where they made you eat boiled vegetables and you had to learn to manage your anger. And TJ's dad would pay a hired killer to climb over the wire at night and strangle me in my bed.

TJ took a final drag, stubbed his fag out on the window frame and pinged the butt over the hedge into the neighbours' pond. 'You must be the most anti-social family I have ever met. I mean, it's not like I've got bubonic plague or anything.'

'True,' I said. 'If you'd got bubonic plague, there'd be bunting everywhere and we'd be drinking champagne.'

Then I legged it.

A couple of hours later I was lying in the bath looking at the Reverend MacGooley's famous photograph of the Loch Ness monster taken just north of Fort Augustus in 1957, and wondering whether it was real or not, whether you could rig up something like that with a dead seal and a couple of water wings. Suddenly the door burst open.

This was a bit of a surprise since the door was locked. I opened my eyes and blew away the suds from round my face. TJ was standing on the bathmat and the bolt was dangling from a broken nail. He wandered over to the loo and sat down on the lid.

'You broke the lock,' I said.

'Correct. Ten points,' he replied.

'Dad is going to kill you.'

'Unlikely,' he said. 'But more about that later . . .'

'Anyway,' I said, 'what the hell are you doing in here? This is *my* bathroom and I'm having a bath and it's private, OK? So get out.'

He smiled to himself. 'I'm afraid there are going to be a few changes around here, Benny-boy.'

'Get . . . Out.'

TJ ignored me completely. 'A certain person is going to have to start being a lot more friendly to me . . . And that person is you.'

There was a Sainsbury's bag on his lap and an evil, self-satisfied look on his face.

'Been giving your room the once-over,' he said. 'Came up with some very interesting stuff indeed . . . And I'm not talking about your Mickey Mouse underpants.'

'I hate you,' I said quietly. 'I hate you more than you will ever know.'

'Nope,' he continued, cheerily, 'the really interesting stuff was *this*.'

He reached into the Sainsbury's bag and pulled out a photograph of Barney, Jenks and me sitting on the sofa in the Command Centre wearing our Z badges.

This was not good.

I gritted my teeth and decided to call TJ's bluff.

'OK,' I said. 'Your time's up. I want the bathroom back now. So move it. And if you think you can blackmail me into being nice to you with a stupid photograph then you've got a kidney bean for a brain.'

TJ chuckled in a worryingly relaxed way. 'Of course I'm not going to blackmail you with those photographs, Ben.' He whipped something else out of the bag. 'I'm going to blackmail you with *this*.'

My heart sank. It was the video. *Breezeblock Comes a Cropper*. Labelled in *my* handwriting, with a big red Z on the cover.

I realized too late that I really should have pushed TJ out of the window, high security hospital or no high security hospital.

I lunged at the video. TJ whipped it out of my reach. 'Of course, I didn't realize *quite* how funny it was until I asked your mum who Breezeblock was.'

'You showed it to *Mum* . . . !?'

'Nah. We were just chatting. About school and stuff. And Breezeblock happened to come up in the conversation.' TJ was talking in that calm, detached voice that villains use in films when they are about to lower someone into the acid tank. 'She knows nothing. Neither does your dad. Or Mrs Block, for that matter. And they're going to carry on knowing nothing. Do you know why, Ben . . . ? Because you are going to crawl. You are going to crawl like you have never crawled in your life. And the first piece of crawling that you are going to do is to apologize nicely to your father for having broken the lock on the bathroom door.'

'But I didn't break it,' I said without thinking.

TJ shook his head despairingly and made a little tutting noise, then ripped the loo-roll holder off the wall as well.

'Oh dear, Ben,' he said, 'look what you've done now. You really are a very clumsy boy, aren't you?' He smiled and waggled the videotape at me, just out of reach. Then he tucked it under his arm and stood up. 'Ah, yes, I almost forgot. A mug of hot chocolate on my bedside table in about ten minutes would be much appreciated. And, erm . . . a bike, I think.'

'A bike?'

'Well, I don't want to be stuck in this dump all the time, do I? And as for walking to school . . .'

'A *bike*?'

'Your mountain bike will be fine. But I'll need the mud cleaning off. I'll need the tyres pumping up properly. I'll need the chrome polishing. And I'll need the saddle raising about ten centimetres. Let's say . . . by nine o'clock tomorrow morning? Oh, and one last thing.'

'What?'

'I would like you to call me "Sir".'

He leant over the bath, patted my head and disappeared through the door, closing it behind him.

I felt like Ken did in *Dalston Junction*, when he looked up from the bottom of the big hole on the building site and saw Danny unloading two tons of gravel on top of him and he knew he was going to die and they cut a fraction of a second beforehand and went into the

44

adverts. Except that if I knew I was going to die I'd be relieved. Because then I wouldn't have to be TJ's slave. And, anyway, Ken wasn't really dead because his real name was Christopher Palmer and he got killed because he'd just released a single which had got to the top of the charts and he was going off to be a pop star and make millions, so I was a lot deader than him by a long chalk.

I closed my eyes and sank down beneath the suds.

There was something lumpy in the bath. I jumped in surprise and sat up, sloshing soapy water all over the bathroom floor. Gingerly, I slid my hands down beside my leg and retrieved the lumpy thing.

It was an almost completely dissolved copy of *The Loch Ness Monster: Fact or Fiction?*

Bananas of the Lost Ark

Mum perched on the lawnmower. 'How on *earth* did it happen?'

I pulled the sleeping bag up around my chin and tried to look as ill as possible. 'It was the mushroom soup, I think.'

'The mushroom soup?'

'There were these shooting pains in my stomach and I just had to rush to the loo. So I sprinted upstairs and ran along the landing and . . .'

'Kicked the door down?'

'Yes. No. I mean, TJ was in there, you see. But I thought it was empty, so I just shoved the door open and the lock came off . . .'

'And the loo-roll holder . . . ?'

'Well, TJ was a bit surprised, obviously, and there was a bit of a scuffle . . .'

'And I don't suppose this is connected to you lending him your new mountain bike. Your brand new mountain bike that you wouldn't even let Jenks borrow . . .'

'Well, erm . . . You know, I just thought I'd encourage him to spend as much time out of the house as possible.'

Mum looked me straight in the eye. 'You're up to something, aren't you?'

'No.'

'Well,' Mum continued, 'seeing as you're so terribly ill, you'd better lie here for the rest of the day and read books quietly.' She smiled sweetly at me. 'I'll bring a spare blanket down to keep you warm. And incidentally . . .'

'What?'

'Next time you get shooting pains in your stomach, *knock*, OK? Because if *I'm* in the bathroom, there'll be more than a scuffle.'

'Promise.'

Mum disappeared and I slipped down under the top of the sleeping bag. I closed my eyes and the Torture Attic materialized slowly before me. In the centre of the dingy room I could just make out the figure of TJ, strapped down to the slicing table by the tight, brass cuffs which flashed and glittered in the light of the burning brands fixed to the stone walls.

'Start the saw,' I said to the fanged hunchback.

He pulled the cobwebbed lever and the rusty engine coughed into life. The whirring blade rose ominously into the gap between TJ's legs and began inching towards him, the steel teeth glinting in the torchglow, sparks flying from the grinding metal cogs.

TJ began to scream.

'Full speed,' I said to the hunchback. 'Let's slice him.'

'Of course, Master,' he replied, baring his twisty yellow teeth. He yanked the lever down another three notches. 'Nothing would give me greater pleasure.'

'Please! No! Help! Save me! Stop! Ben! I'll do anything! Anything! Just stop this thing! Please!' cried TJ, sweat pouring from his face, his eyes rolling back in their sockets.

It was too late. I couldn't even hear him any longer. The noise of the blades was too loud.

Three centimetres. Two centimetres. One centimetre.

Steel met flesh. Shrieking. Grating. Sparks. Smoke.

Blood sprayed across the screen and dripped slowly away to reveal the words GOODBYE TJ . . . DR BEN WINS AGAIN . . . HA HA HA HA HA!

Mum dropped in around one o'clock carrying an invalid's lunch on a tray. I was halfway through the boiled eggs and toast soldiers when she said, casually, 'I almost forgot. Barney rang to ask you to come round to his house. I explained that I'd poisoned you with a bowl of mushroom soup and you'd gone mad and started smashing things in the bathroom and we were keeping you under close observation until you returned to normal.'

'And what did Barney say?'

'He said, "You have a wicked sense of humour, Mrs

Simpson," and told me that you could see *Bananas of the Lost Ark* some other time.'

'*Bananas of the Lost Ark?*'

'Search me,' said Mum.

'Actually,' I said, 'I've been feeling a lot better over the last hour or two.' I began shovelling the second boiled egg down as fast as it would go. 'See. My appetite's coming back.'

'Ben . . .'

'Plus, I think it'd be good for me if I got some fresh air.' I wriggled out of the sleeping bag and stood up. 'You know. Rather than being cooped up all day in here.'

Mum shook her head. 'Well *that's* a surprise.'

'Maybe it wasn't your mushroom soup, after all,' I said, feeling perkier already. 'Maybe it was an allergy to TJ. Er, don't tell him I said that, will you?'

Mum shook her head and raised her eyebrows at me.

'Cracking lunch,' I said, handing her the plate. 'I'm feeling miles better already. Bye!'

I leapt through the shed door and sprinted up the garden to get my bike. Then I remembered that it wasn't my bike any more. I kicked a gnome and headed off to Barney's on foot.

'Ben! Hey! I thought you were dead. Come in.'

'I *am* dead,' I said, following Barney through to his lounge, 'but it's a long story.'

He vaulted the back of the sofa and landed in a TV-watching slump. I walked round the normal way and sat down, on account of being in a depressed, non-vaulting mood.

'Rewind?' asked Jenks.

'Yep,' said Barney, 'let's take it from the top.'

The video whirred. On screen, a bearded man in an orange boiler suit was being glued down to a large wooden board with Griptex Supertight©.

'This is just an old advert at the beginning of the tape,' explained Jenks.

Four burly men turned the large wooden board upside down and it was whisked into the air by a waiting helicopter. They cut to a shot of the man suspended hundreds of metres above Central London then zoomed in for a close-up. 'Would you trust any other glue to do *this*?' he shouted.

'Here we are,' said Jenks, hitting PLAY.

The screen was filled with white noise, then the opening title, BANANAS OF THE LOST ARK, marker-penned in red onto an orange cardboard background, ANOTHER THRILLING FILM FROM Z PRODUCTIONS . . . STARRING . . . HARRISON BANANA.

The titles were whipped away and behind them was a shot of Barney's own dining room. Accompanying this scene was a cheesy tune played on an electric organ. Nothing was happening in the dining room and nothing carried on happening for some considerable time.

'It's gripping,' I said.

'Be patient,' said Barney.

Slowly the camera began to close in on the dining table. In the centre of the table was a large, wooden fruit-bowl containing three pears, four apples, a bunch of slightly withered grapes and a single banana. Under the cheesy organ tune you could just hear the faint sound of the *Jaws* theme building slowly.

Suddenly, the banana started to move. Just a twitch or two at first. The *Jaws* theme began to drown out the organ. The banana started to wriggle out from between the kiwis. Then, with one terrifying, muscular hotch, it levered itself over the rim of the fruit-bowl and down onto the surface of the table. The camera tracked it as it made its way to the edge of the table, over the edge, down one of the legs and across the carpet towards the door.

At the door it stopped and reared up on its pointy banana-bottom. A small, slitty mouth opened up on its inner curve and an evil chuckle bubbled out before it dropped to the floor once more and disappeared into the hallway.

Another card appeared reading THE END. Jenks hit the STOP button on the video and Channel 4 reappeared. 'Here, in this bucket,' said a beardy scientist, 'is just a selection of the sewage we found on this popular tourist beach this morning.'

Jenks turned the TV off.

'What do you think?' asked Jenks.

'I'm impressed,' I said. And I *was* impressed. 'How did you do it?'

'Well, David,' said Barney, leaning back and smoking an imaginary cigar. 'A magnet or two. A bit of cotton here and there. Some stop-action animation. You know . . . take a frame, move the banana, take another frame. And three days of sheer hard work. Then I got my Aunt Jennifer to do the soundtrack on her Yamaha electric piano. She's the one who does all those singalongs at old people's homes. Spliced it all together and *Hey Presto!*'

'Yeah,' said Jenks, 'and we were thinking, like, we'd do this horror film with bananas in and they'd be aliens who came from outer space who looked like bananas and killed everyone and took over the whole planet . . .'

'Or,' added Barney, 'they could be normal bananas which have been exposed to gamma rays in a laboratory, or had their genetic structure mucked about with. Or there could be a scientist who's invented a matter transport machine and it's like in *The Fly*, except it's not a fly which gets caught in the machine with him but a banana in his packed lunch. And when he transports himself their atoms get all mixed up and he's turned into a human banana and the banana's turned into . . .'

Me, I was thinking about TJ. About him nicking my bike. About having to make him hot chocolate all the time. About having to run back and forth to the shops to get him Mars Bars and cans of Coke and motorcycle magazines. About having to be nice to him all the time. And I was thinking about Breezeblock. Whether she was in traction on an orthopaedic ward in the General Hospital. How the three of us could be banged up for GBH if TJ so much as breathed a word . . .

'Ben . . . ? Ben . . . ?' Barney rapped on my forehead with his knuckles.

'Hello? Oh yeah. Sorry.'

'What's up?' he asked.

'Oh, nothing. It's just that . . . well . . . you know the Breezeblock video?'

'Yeah.'

'TJ found it. He went through my bag. Before I had a chance to hide it. And he found this picture of us in the Command Centre. Wearing our Z badges. Like the Queen. On the fiver.'

Barney gave me a very dark look indeed.

'And he's threatening to show it to everyone. Mum, Dad, Breezeblock . . .'

'Ah,' said Barney.

'. . . unless I make him hot chocolate all the time and call him "Sir" and run errands and give him my bike and be crawlingly nice to him all the time. Plus, his mum and dad are going to be away for at least a month, so he's got to come to school as well and . . .'

'Let me get this straight,' said Barney. 'If you do all these things . . . the hot chocolate, the "Sir" thing, the errands, the bike, the being nice . . . then he won't show the video to anyone?'

'Yeah.'

'Well,' said Barney. 'There seems to be one obvious answer to that.'

'What?'

'You give him the bike, Ben,' he said. 'You call him "Sir". You run those errands. You make that hot chocolate extra creamy and you treat him like the Sultan of Brunei.'

'Thanks a million.'

Barney shook my hand. 'I knew we could trust you, kid.'

Big Fight, Red Ink, Inflatable Bananas

Monday was the first day back at school.

First Days Back At School are never good. But this one turned out to be particularly grim when Breezeblock limped onto the podium at assembly with one foot in plaster and the infamous fiver in her hand.

She told everyone the story of how she had been the victim of a cruel prank in the Grosvenor Centre. The prank was, she suspected, the work of 'some unpleasant and brainless children'. She then held the fiver up and said that if *anyone* knew *anything* about who was behind this 'appalling outrage' they should come and talk to her in confidence.

Jenks swallowed so hard it sounded as if he was eating billiard balls.

On the bright side, TJ got into a fight with Fisty Morgan during lunch-hour, which was immensely satisfying.

Fisty is a homicidal maniac a couple of years above us. He should be four years above us but his brain would fuse if he had to do things like long division. He's been shaving since the age of eight and can open beer-bottles with his teeth. He has a home-made tattoo of a skull on his forearm and head-butts teachers whenever the opportunity arises.

Barney, Jenks and I were sitting on the wall outside the science block at the time, digesting our fishfingers and strawberry mousse and discussing ways in which bananas might mutate and pose a threat to the future of humanity. Suddenly, a crowd of jostling kids poured round the corner shouting, 'Fight! Fight! Fight!'

We slipped off the wall, wandered over to the mob and eased ourselves between the spectators to see what was happening.

'Who is it?' I asked a small boy with a brace and a Man Utd badge.

'Some new kid,' he said. 'Started chatting up Gail Forrester. You know, Fisty Morgan's girlfriend. Now Fisty's killing him.'

We pushed on into the jostling centre of the throng. I didn't realize the new boy was TJ until the bodies parted and I found myself looking down onto a small circle of earth where Fisty was trying to turn my cousin's face into a puree. A cheering sight, indeed.

'Fight! Fight! Fight!' cheered the crowd.

DFFF! went TJ's boot against Fisty's shin.

56

DNK! went Fisty's fist against TJ's head.

To give him his due, TJ was giving Fisty a good run for his money. True, TJ is older by a couple of years, but Mr Lanchester is thirty-four and he'd ended up in Casualty after his little bout with Fisty in the dining-hall queue last year.

'So, this is your famous cousin?' said Barney, who hadn't yet seen TJ.

'Yep,' I said.

'In which case . . .' said Barney. 'If you'll allow me . . .' He glanced round to check whether any of Fisty's cronies were in the crowd, then took the top off one of his three fountain pens, unscrewed the body, squeezed the rubber cartridge and sprayed TJ's head with a jet of bright, red ink. Thankfully both Fisty and TJ were too preoccupied with trying to murder each other to notice who had done this.

'Think of it as a present,' said Barney, putting his pen back together and slipping it into his pocket, 'from me to you.'

'Thanks,' I said.

'My pleasure.'

We carried on watching the fight for a few more minutes until Barney turned to me and said, 'I've been thinking. How about this . . . ? There's an accident, OK. At a nuclear power plant. Like Chernobyl. And, by chance, this greengrocer's lorry is driving past when it goes up. There's this crate of bananas in the back and . . .'

'How are we going to show a nuclear power plant going up?' I asked.

'We get videos from the library. Record stuff off the telly. We don't have to get film of a nuclear power plant blowing up *as such*. We just need film of a nuclear power plant. Film of dials going into the red. Film of something glowing red hot. Film of an explosion. Film of a mushroom cloud. We transfer it to the digital camcorder and splice it all together on the computer.'

At which point, Mr Lanchester strode through the crowd, with Potato-Head Dawson in tow, pushing everyone aside and shouting, 'Stop this ridiculous behaviour at once!'

He had reached the middle of the scrum and was about to bend down and make an attempt at separating the two boys when he saw that one of them was covered in a pint of red ink and realized that if he got stuck in he could end up making a trip, not just to the staffroom medical cupboard, but to the dry cleaner's as well.

'Don't worry, Bob,' said Potato-Head, 'they'll soon dry off thrashing around like this. We'll just stand around and wait until they've worn themselves out.'

Lanchester glared at him. This was not the kind of joke you were meant to make in front of the pupils. He turned to the crowd and yelled, 'Come on. Move it. The show's over.'

But the show wasn't over and they had to do exactly what Potato-Head suggested they do and wait till Fisty and TJ got bored. But Fisty and TJ were pretty keen on this kind of thing and were still going strong when the break-bell rang and we trooped back inside.

*

On the way home from school I was passing Reggie's Veggies when Mum appeared at the door holding an aubergine, saying, 'Sorry, Ben. I forgot to put the key under the gnome. You're locked out, I'm afraid. Fancy coming in and helping me carry some of this stuff back to the ranch?'

I stepped inside.

'Hi there, Ben,' said Belinda, brushing her long, blonde hair out of her face and sliding her scissors back into the pocket of her stripy, green apron. She picked up a crate of new potatoes. 'How's my favourite little customer?'

'Er. Yeah. All right,' I said, examining the toe of my shoes.

'Your mum was telling me you've been sleeping in the shed, you poor thing.'

'Yeah,' I replied, examining the ceiling.

'On account of this horrible cousin of yours taking over your bedroom.'

'Yeah.' I glanced round to hide the fact that I was blushing and, as I turned round, I saw two large bananas hanging from the ceiling in the far corner of the shop.

Bingo!

'Are you OK, Ben?' asked Belinda.

'Er . . . I was just thinking.'

'What?'

'Those bananas. Up there. The big plastic ones.'

'Yes?'

'Where do you get them from?'

'From the banana wholesalers. Why? Do you want them?'

'Well . . . I mean . . . Big plastic bananas could come in really useful over the next couple of weeks.'

'Well, since it's you,' she said, and winked at me.

'I mean, if that's OK.'

'You do have some strange hobbies, Ben,' said Mum.

Belinda dragged the stool over to the root vegetable section and climbed onto it. 'Reg was going to take them down tomorrow,' she said, scissoring the cotton that held the bananas up. 'We got these blow-up carrots delivered the other day and he reckoned they'd make a change. So these would only go in the bin.' She got down off the stool and handed me the bananas. 'There you go.'

'Er . . . Brilliant . . . Thanks.'

Mum was emptying the shopping and I was leaning against the table holding the two six-foot bananas when she said, 'So, how did your darling cousin get on at school today?'

'Actually,' I said, 'there's a faint possibility that he might actually be in hospital at this very moment. But I wouldn't get your hopes up.'

'Meaning . . .'

'He and Fisty Morgan. They had this fight. It was brilliant. Everyone was watching. They were still fighting when we went back inside after lunch.'

But TJ wasn't in hospital, because he came through the front door two seconds later and headed straight for the stairs, shouting, 'Ben! Up here now!'

Mum gave me a puzzled look.

'Better humour him,' I said, dumping the bananas and wandering out of the kitchen.

When I got upstairs, TJ was naked from the waist up, leaning over the bathroom sink scrubbing at his face with a soapy flannel. His ink-splattered white shirt was draped over the cistern.

'I need a new shirt,' he said.

'Oh dear. How did that happen?' I said, as caringly as I could manage. 'Sir.'

'Shut your face and shut it now,' said TJ, scrubbing away at his face. 'I need a new shirt. Same size as that one. You've got twenty minutes.'

He stood up from the sink and looked into the mirror. His face was the colour of a postbox and the soap really wasn't doing much to change this.

'And something to get this stuff off,' he growled.

'Like what?'

'Use your imagination, Einstein.'

'But . . . I mean . . . How am I going to pay for all this . . . ? Sir.'

'You've got twenty quid in that stupid Darth Vader bank on your windowsill.'

'That's *my* money . . . Sir. And there's forty quid in there, actually . . . Sir.'

'Not any more there isn't.'

'You . . . !'

He grabbed hold of my jacket lapels and pressed his ugly, sud-covered, vermillion face up against mine. 'I've got the video, snot-face. So if I tell you to turn the food processor on and put your head in, you do it, right? Don't push me, kid.'

I picked up the ink-stained shirt, turned and went to my bedroom, removed the last two tenners from the Darth Vader bank and headed out to the shops.

On the way I imagined dropping him overboard somewhere off the Great Barrier Reef, roped to a string bag of raw beefsteaks, the shadow of a Great White approaching through the dark blue water, rising underneath his dangling legs, surfacing in an explosion of spray and tearing his body to ribbons in its muscular, razor-filled jaws.

That made me feel a little better.

I bought a new white shirt from Bagnells and a tub of Swarfega paint cleaner from the chemist.

I was in the chemist's when I had the brainwave. Using

my last two pounds I bought a tube of Veet hair remover. I sat down on a bench outside the shop, opened the Swarfega, added the tube of hair remover, gave it a good stir with an old biro, chucked the biro and the empty tube of Veet, put the lid back on the Swarfega and headed home with a spring in my step.

Your Friend the Atom

I delivered the shirt and the Swarfega to TJ and came back downstairs. The *Dalston Junction* theme tune was playing, so I went into the lounge, shoved Badger off the sofa and settled myself down next to Mum. She opened a new box of Belgian chocolates, removed all the white chocolate truffles, arranged them in a little pyramid within easy reach of her right hand on the arm of the sofa then offered the box to me.

I selected a hazelnut praline.

The theme tune died away and the camera panned across a graveyard to show Ken's funeral procession. The coffin was being carried in the bucket of Danny's JCB on account of Ken being a builder. Unfortunately Danny wasn't very good at operating the JCB, which was why he'd accidentally killed Ken in the first place. So it was par for the course when he got his sleeve caught on the bucket lever and spilled Ken's coffin onto the gravel.

The coffin fell open, everyone gasped and they cut to the Blue Lagoon Bar 'n' Grill where Benny was serving Ronnie Ahmed when his new toupee came unstuck and fell into Ronnie's chicken risotto.

I thought at first that it was Ronnie screaming but it wasn't. It was TJ.

'What on earth . . . ?' said Mum, jumping to her feet and heading for the door. Pausing briefly, she turned and pointed at her pyramid of white chocolate truffles and said, 'Look after those.'

I glanced at Badger. He was fast asleep under the dining table. Or pretending to be fast asleep. Hell, it didn't matter. Nothing was going to stop me seeing what was going on upstairs.

When I reached the landing I could see Mum and TJ having a stand-off in the bathroom.

'Do you mind telling me what is going on?' asked Mum.

TJ turned and gave me the sort of look you get from dogs with rabies. His face was back to its normal pasty flesh colour. But his eyebrows were missing.

'What in heaven's name have you done to yourself?' said Mum.

There was also a large bald patch over his left ear. He looked down at the jar of Swarfega in his hand and glared at it. 'But . . . but . . .'

Mum put her hands on her hips. 'Frankly, TJ, if you will try to wash your face with paint-cleaner, you really can't complain when it all goes horribly wrong.'

You could actually hear his teeth grinding together.

'Honestly,' said Mum, shaking her head. 'I've got better things to do than stand around here watching you trying to make yourself look like the Bride of Frankenstein.' She swivelled and headed downstairs to watch the remainder of *Dalston Junction*.

I stepped towards TJ. Close, but not within punching distance. I said, 'Are you OK? Sir?'

He gritted his teeth at me. '*Don't call me "Sir"!*'

'But you asked me to call you "Sir", Sir.'

'Well, I'm telling you to stop it. Now.'

'Yes, Sir.'

TJ lunged at me and got his hands round my neck and pinned me to the bathroom door.

I said, as politely as I could, 'If I could make a sugges-
tion . . . *gnk* . . . If you want to get rid of the rest of your
hair . . . *nnrkg* . . . You know, shave it off . . . *nrkgnk* . . .
You could use Mum's shaver . . . *kkkrg* . . .'

I pointed to the top of the cupboard where Mum's
newly-mended pink Ladyshave was sitting on its
recharger-unit.

That was when we heard the second scream. From
downstairs this time.

I took advantage of the momentary distraction to squirm
free from TJ's grip and leg it to the lounge where Mum
was berating Badger for having scoffed all her truffles.

True, I had to spend the rest of the evening soaping
white chocolate-flavoured dog-sick out of the carpet but
it was better than getting strangled.

Plus, there was the compensatory entertainment of the
third scream when the Ladyshave exploded again and
dug itself into TJ's head.

'I think we should put TJ in the film,' I said.

'Yeah,' said Jenks, excitedly, 'and have him killed by
mutant killer bananas.'

'Exactly,' I agreed.

'Are you out of your mind?' asked Barney.

'No, listen,' I said. 'You don't actually have to have
him being killed by the bananas. You just have a shot
of him sitting on the sofa. Then you have another shot
of the bananas creeping across the carpet. Then you hear
this scream. And then you have a shot of the mutant
killer bananas dragging the body away. Except it's not

really TJ. It's someone else dressed up as TJ. Or just his empty clothes because they've eaten him alive. And you just edit the shots together afterwards, so TJ wouldn't even know he was in the film. Clever, eh?'

'Who's that with Fisty?' said Jenks, looking over my shoulder. 'The bald weirdo with no eyebrows and the sticking plasters all over his head.'

I turned round to look.

TJ and Fisty's fight had obviously been a kind of bonding experience, because the two of them were standing together on the far side of the playground, beating up small boys, emptying their schoolbags all over the tarmac and stealing their dinner money. The normal Fisty Morgan playtime operation.

'It's TJ.'

'But . . .' said Jenks.

So I told them the story about the hair remover and the Ladyshave and felt pretty smug about it until Barney turned and stared at me and said, in a most unamused way, 'Does he know it was you?'

'No.'

'Good. Because if you do something like that again and he finds out and gives that video to Mrs Block, I am personally going to disembowel you.'

'Hey!' I complained. 'You try sleeping in the shed and not having a bike and having to run his baths and clean his room which is actually *my* room and do his washing up and having to tell Mum that it was *me* who nicked all her chocolate Hob-Nobs. Actually, I think I deserve a medal for not cracking up.'

'OK, OK,' said Barney, backing off.

'Hey,' grinned Jenks. 'Show him the vid and stuff.'

Barney slapped himself on the forehead. 'I completely forgot.' He opened his bag and pulled out a video of *Meltdown!* a thriller about an accident in an American nuclear missile silo, together with a pile of library books about nuclear power. 'Brilliant, eh?'

'But you can't use books, can you?' I asked.

'Course we can,' said Barney, flicking through an ancient hardback called *Your Friend the Atom* and showing me a photo of the Sizewell B power plant. 'These can be stills. We can cut between the two. It'll look a bit odd. But that's really cool and post-modern. At least I think it's post-modern. And one of us can be the van-driver delivering the bananas and we'll have this shot of you or me or Jenks sitting behind the wheel and looking terrified and then the power station blows up and we see this mushroom cloud and suddenly there's this blinding white light which fills the cab and the driver screams and dies and collapses onto the steering wheel. And then we see the mutated bananas escaping from the back of the van . . .'

It sounded good.

'Now all we need,' said Barney, 'is a van.'

'Oh yeah. *I* forgot something, too,' I said. 'I was in Reggie's Veggies the other day and I got these two huge, plastic bananas. I was thinking maybe we could use them as the ringleader-bananas. You know, the really, *really* radioactively mutated ones who are in charge of taking over the planet.'

'Reggie's Veggies!' shouted Barney. 'Why didn't *I* think of that. Of course! They've got a van. And that Belinda who works in there. She's got a bit of a soft-spot for you, hasn't she? Ben, you're a genius. Look. All you have to do is butter her up a bit. Explain that we're making this film and ask whether we can use the van. Just for a few minutes. It doesn't even have to go anywhere. We could even offer her a role in the film if she's on for it . . .'

'Hang on a minute,' I said. 'We can't just . . . I mean . . . That's not fair . . .'

'A person of your charm and good looks,' said Barney, 'will have her wrapped round your little finger.'

'And if she stars in the film,' sniggered Jenks, 'there could be this scene where the two of you snog and . . .'

'Jenks,' said Barney, flatly, 'get real, OK?'

'Look . . .' I said.

Barney sidled up to me and slid his arm around my shoulder and said, in an elder brother kind of way, 'Ben. This is important. Remember the Agent Z Code of Honour . . .'

At four o'clock, the three of us walked into Reggie's Veggies, me in front, being pushed, Barney behind me doing the pushing, and Jenks following on behind, chortling.

Belinda was on the far side of the till, doing an avocado arrangement on blue tissue paper.

'Go on,' said Barney.

'Er . . . excuse me,' I croaked.

Belinda stood up and turned round and said, sharply, 'What?' She did not look happy.

'Hi, Belinda . . . I . . . um . . .'

'Oh, hullo, Ben. Sorry. I didn't realize it was you. I didn't mean to bite your head off. It's not been a good day.'

'Oh . . . yeah . . . Right . . . Really?'

Belinda wandered back to the till. 'Reg did his back in moving a potato sack this morning and I've had to run the place on my own. Then we had the plumbers in to do the sink out the back. And I've just spent the last ten minutes being chatted up by some poisonous little twerp with a shaved head and sticking plasters all over it who thought he was God's gift to women and kept calling me a babe.'

'Sorry.'

'Sorry?'

'Yeah, sorry. I mean . . .' I was blushing again. 'That was TJ. My cousin. You know. The one who's staying with us.'

'*That* was TJ?' She swept her hair out of her face and popped a grape into her mouth. 'Well, Ben, you have my deepest sympathy. Frankly, I would have killed him by now if he was living in my house.'

'Yeah, so would I. Except he is. And I haven't. I mean . . .'

She smiled at me and shook her head. 'Anyway, what can I do for you?'

'Well . . . I . . . That is *we* . . . We . . . Well, this is going to sound pretty stupid . . . That's because it *is* pretty stupid actually . . .'

Barney pushed me aside and said, 'Honestly. All the cuteness and none of the patter. What a waste.' He turned to Belinda and took a deep breath. 'We . . . Ben, Jenks and I . . . Jenks, put that celery down . . . Ben, Jenks and I are making a film. A science fiction thriller. It's going to be a fairly low-budget production. But most of the best films *are* low-budget these days, in my opinion. And what we need to get our hands on at this precise moment in time is a greengrocer's van for the opening sequence. Which is where you come in. Hopefully. We don't need anything fancy. One shot showing the van going down a country road. One shot of the driver seen through the windscreen. And a few slightly more complicated shots of the back doors. Of course, if you wanted to be in the opening scene yourself, well, we'd be extremely flattered. That goes without saying. The person driving the van does die, but they die in this really tasteful way, no horrible injuries or anything.'

'You're making a *film*?' asked Belinda, sceptically.

'And of course the best bit,' continued Barney, getting a bit inventive, 'is that, at the climax, Ben's cousin TJ is going to get killed by these monsters.'

'I'll just take these parsnips,' said an elderly lady in a furry, purple beret.

'Monsters?' said Belinda, weighing the parsnips. 'That'll be eighty-four pence, please, Mrs Chiselford.'

'Radiation-mutated homicidal bananas,' explained Barney, as if radiation-mutated homicidal bananas were the most natural thing in the world.

'Cheerio,' said Mrs Chiselford.

'Bananas?'

'Er . . . yeah.'

'And how precisely are these bananas going to kill Ben's cousin?' she asked sceptically.

'Still working on that one,' nodded Barney, sagely. 'I find that I prefer to keep the script fluid while we're filming. Gives it a kind of loose, organic feel.'

Belinda stared at Barney for several seconds. 'You three are completely mad.'

'No,' said Barney, 'TJ is mad. What we are is creative and eccentric and just that little bit different from your average kid.'

'And we'll buy loads of bananas,' I added helpfully, 'as extras.'

She pondered the matter while serving a bag of swedes, radishes and clementines to a man with a Jack Russell. Finally, she said, 'I am probably going to regret this, but . . . Well, it just happens to be your lucky week. Reg normally drives the van, but what with his back being out, I'm borrowing it this weekend . . . You know Somersby Road, the one that goes to Blackthorn, just past the ringroad? Number 57. It's my boyfriend's house. Roger. I'll be there on Sunday morning. 10 o'clock, OK?'

'That's just utterly, utterly brilliant,' I drivelled. 'You're . . . erm . . . I . . .'

'You're extremely generous,' said Barney, more suavely.

'I'm a sucker, that's what I am,' said Belinda. 'Just one thing . . .'

'What?' asked Barney.

'I do hope that this isn't some kind of unpleasant practical joke.'

'Practical joke?' asked Barney with mock-flabbergastedness.

'It's just that I remember Ben's mum saying something about you putting slices of carrot in the fish-tank at the doctor's surgery and hoicking them out and pretending they were goldfish and eating them and causing a small riot.'

'No, no, no,' said Barney, 'you've got the wrong end of the stick completely.'

'Er, completely,' I agreed.

'She would have been talking about *Den*,' said Barney. 'Ben's cousin. Always getting into trouble.'

'What unpleasant cousins you have,' said Belinda, raising her eyebrows at me just like Mum.

'Yeah,' I said, fiddling with a grapefruit.

'Total headache,' said Barney. 'Ran off to join the Foreign Legion eventually. Bit of a relief for all concerned. Anyway, see you on Sunday at ten. Ciao!'

When I got home, the kitchen door was wide open and TJ was doing press-ups on the patio to make himself more attractive to babes. There was a cloud of armpit pong drifting into the house.

'A lemon squash would do nicely, Ben,' he grunted. 'Forty-one. Ooof. Forty-two. Ooof. Forty-three. Ooof.'

'Coming right up, Sir . . .' I paused. 'Erm . . . By the way. Am I still meant to be calling you "Sir"?'

74

'Just get us the squash, you berk.'

I opened the fridge, fixed him a big tumbler, stood it next to his stinky biceps and wandered down the garden feeling rather jolly on account of having survived the encounter at Reggie's Veggies.

'Blu-ue Moooooon!' sang Elvis as I pushed open the shed door. 'You saw me standing alone . . .'

Dad was wearing his drainpipe trousers and a lot of hair gel. He was de-rusting his socket-set and generally keeping a low profile until it was time to make a quick getaway to the Plasterer's Arms for his Rock 'n' Roll night.

'Greetings, Mighty Parent-Person!' I said, moving my two large, plastic bananas to one side, taking out Dr Scream's House of Horror and settling myself down on the sleeping bag.

I flipped straight to the Torture Attic and zapped open the secret panel in the woodwork. I stepped into the hidden lift, zapped the gargoyle and zoomed down three floors. The panel slid open again. The words SO YOU HAVE FOUND THE WAY INTO MY SECRET LAIR AT LONG LAST appeared on the screen and then dripped away to reveal the silhouette of Dr Scream himself, back-lit by flames rising from the mouths of two stone wolves. NO ONE IS ALLOWED TO SEE THE FACE OF DR SCREAM. PREPARE TO DIE.

'Something's up, isn't it?' said Dad.

'Is it?' I asked casually.

'The hot chocolate,' said Dad. He had his serious voice on, so I hit PAUSE and looked up. 'The lemon squash. The bike. The errands. This being-nice-to-TJ rubbish. I thought you hated him.'

'I do.'

'I'm not blind, Ben. And I'm not stupid. And you're not that keen on chocolate Hob-Nobs.'

'Without a dream in my heart,' sang Elvis. 'Without a love of my own.'

Dad put his hands behind his head and looked up at the ceiling and became all dreamy and reminiscent and began talking really slowly, like dads do when they're in that we-need-to-have-a-friendly-discussion mood. 'When I was thirteen, Ben . . .'

'Can't we talk about football, or something?' I suggested, vainly.

'No, we can't. I'm having a fatherly chat with you. Which I don't do very often. So I am going to make the most of it.' I kept my mouth shut. 'When I was thirteen there was this little kid who used to live next door. Christopher Smith. Glasses. Spots. Skinny. You know the type. Anyway, his mum used to bring him round to our house sometimes so she and your gran could have a good old chinwag. And I thought it was great fun to terrorize this poor boy. I used to hang him upside down out of windows and say I was going to drop him. That sort of thing. I put him in the oven once and completely forgot about him, and your gran came within an inch of cooking him . . . Got a good thrashing for that, I can tell you.'

'Jeez, you really *were* horrible before you met Mum, weren't you?'

'Funny thing is, I met him again, about twelve years later. I was at the dentist, having a couple of fillings done, and I looked up at this bloke revving his drill and he said, 'You're Trevor Simpson, aren't you?' And it was him. And I can honestly say that they were the most painful fillings I have ever had in my life. Quite right, too, really. I deserved every minute of it. Though, I have to say, we did change dentists pretty quickly after that.'

'Dad . . .'

'I'm getting there, Ben. I'm getting there. The point is . . . I know how people like TJ operate. And I know how people like you operate. And people like you don't go around bowing and scraping to people like TJ without something fishy going on. So I think you'd better spill the beans.'

'It's nothing,' I said. 'Honestly. Nothing.'

'Right,' he said, 'if you won't tell me what's going on, I'll ask TJ.'

'*No!*' I squeaked.

Dad stared at me in a stern but kindly way. 'Ben, it's not *you* I'm cross with, it's TJ.'

It was bean-spilling time. 'OK . . . He's, erm . . . he's sort of blackmailing me.'

Dad frowned. 'Go on.'

I gave him the edited version. We'd played this joke. To do with school. No one was hurt, exactly. And it *was* funny. But TJ found out. And he was going to tell Mrs Block if I didn't do everything he asked.

'It's a Code-of-Honour kind of thing,' I added. 'I can't tell you about it because I promised I wouldn't tell anyone and if I tell you I'll be in even bigger trouble with Barney and Jenks. So I just have to live with it until TJ goes home or gets bored.'

Dad was astonishingly cool about it, actually. He didn't push me for more details. He said he understood about secrets and everything. He said it didn't really matter what Barney, Jenks and I got up to so long as it wasn't illegal or dangerous, and so long as we weren't nasty to other people or cruel to animals.

I tried not to think about Mrs Block's plastered foot. Or the Afghan hound.

He told me about some of the tricks he'd played when he was at school – putting caps in the hinge of their teacher's desk so that it exploded when she dropped the lid; glueing a tiny china frog to the inside of a coffee mug at home so that one of Gran's friends screamed and spat a whole mug of tea over the kitchen wall – and I made a mental note to jot them down in the Suggestions Book at the Command Centre.

Dad said he might not be able to do anything about the blackmail, but he would try and 'even things out a bit', whatever that meant. And all in all, the two of us ended up having a pretty good Quality Time experience, so much so that Dad ended up getting to the Plasterer's Arms an hour late.

When he came back, just before ten o'clock, TJ was sitting at the kitchen table eating a sandwich and Mum was making me a cocoa and a hot water bottle to take down to the shed. Dad had just finished fixing himself a cheese on toast when TJ started taking the mick out of his drainpipe trousers and slicked-back hair. Dad said nothing, just pulled up a chair, suspended one of the legs above TJ's toes, then sat down. Hard. Leaving TJ with a noticeable limp for three days, and leaving me with an extremely warm glow in my stomach.

I climbed into the sleeping bag, arranged my hot water bottle, drank my cocoa and fell asleep almost immediately. Then I dreamt this really weird dream in which I was Dad, and Dad was me. I was married to Belinda who was Mum, and the two of us had been called in after school to discuss the behaviour of our unruly son, Trevor, who had been caught putting caps in the hinges of his teacher's desk.

Mrs Block was silhouetted by two huge flames pouring from the mouths of two stone TJs and growling, 'Welcome to the secret lair of the headmistress, you idiotic parents. YOUR SON HAS BROKEN THE MOST SACRED RULES OF DR BLOCK'S SCHOOL OF FEAR. PREPARE TO DIE. HA HA HA.'

I remember trying to apologize for Dad's behaviour and failing miserably and Belinda turning to me and saying, 'All of the cuteness and none of the patter. What a waste.'

Then Mrs Block mutated into a large plastic banana and everything went black.

Lights! Camera! Action!

We turned up fully equipped at 57 Somersby Road at ten o'clock sharp on Sunday morning. I was carrying the camcorder. Jenks was carrying twenty bananas individually attached to long pieces of fishing twine. And Barney was carrying a huge colour copy of a photograph of Sizewell B nuclear power station which his dad had got enlarged at the office for holding up outside the van window during the driving scenes.

I think Belinda had forgotten all about the filming because she turned up at the door wearing a dressing gown and yawning. Her hair looked like she'd just had an electric shock and she didn't recognize us for a few seconds. But Barney was charming and she told us to come in and help ourselves to some coffee and biscuits while she went and got dressed.

I was pouring out the coffee and Barney was halfway down a packet of Jammy Dodgers when Roger, her boyfriend, appeared in the kitchen looking large and stubbled and unhappy. He asked us who we were and Barney told him we were burglars, but he didn't find this very funny. He told us to hop it. Belinda shouted down from upstairs that he should shut his trap and be nice to us. There was a tense, *Dalston Junction* kind of atmosphere for ten minutes while he ate his way through a plate of sausages and it was quite a relief when Belinda came downstairs again wearing jeans and unelectrocuted hair and we could go outside and start shooting.

I'd never been on a film set before. It was great. We did a few shots of Belinda loading boxes of fruit into the back of the van, a few shots of her climbing into the driving seat and a few shots of her starting the engine and driving away. Then Jenks held up the Sizewell B picture outside the passenger window and Barney wobbled the van while Belinda waggled the steering wheel and I filmed her through the other passenger window with the power station in the background.

Belinda, who was really getting into it by now, said we could make it more realistic if the van was actually moving. So we did the whole scene again with me and Jenks hanging onto the wing mirrors as Belinda drove down Somersby Road at 5 mph. And she was right. It was much more realistic, though Barney had to edit out the bit where Jenks fell off the van and Sizewell B was replaced by a shot of an elderly lady walking her dog who started shouting, 'Help! Someone get an ambulance!' even though Jenks had only twisted his ankle and scabbed his knee a bit.

Then we went back to Number 57 and shot the bit where Belinda looks out of the windscreen and sees the power station exploding and screams and dies and falls onto the steering wheel. There wasn't any blinding white light. But Barney said he could do this later on the computer.

Belinda asked us in for more biscuits and Barney was really crawly and said she'd been brilliant. We'd taken up too much of her time already and would it be possible if we came round to the shop one day next week to film the bananas escaping from the back of the van.

Belinda was just saying how she could probably arrange this when Roger came in looking like death warmed up, grouching about how the two of them were meant to be in the Eight Bells in Shillingford at twelve to meet his mates. Belinda said his mates could go and take a running jump for all she cared. Roger asked how on earth he was going to get there if she wasn't driving him in the van. Belinda told him that if he got off his backside and got himself a job he might be able to afford his own car. As for now, he could go to the pub on Shanks' pony.

'Who's Shanks?' asked Jenks.

'Old guy,' said Barney. 'Lives over in Billing. Rents out small horses.'

Belinda turned to us and said why didn't we film the escaping banana sequence right now. We were much better company than Roger. We knew how to act like gentlemen.

His mates, on the other hand, only wanted to get drunk and go back to Sparky's flat and watch stupid Rugby League on the telly. All of which was very flattering to us but not to Roger, who went a bit red in the face and started swearing loudly and threw all of us out of the house.

This made Belinda rather upset until Barney said, 'Well, at least I got the rest of his Jammy Dodgers and this packet of Fig Rolls,' which made her laugh a little bit. Barney handed everyone a biscuit and we got down to filming again.

Belinda was still a bit depressed, for obvious reasons. So while Barney and Jenks filmed the bananas escaping from the back of the van, I went over and sat with her on the grass verge and gave her my last Fig Roll and said I was sorry for getting her into trouble.

'Oh, that's OK. I was only staying over for the weekend.' She chewed her Fig Roll. 'Besides, I was thinking of giving him the boot anyway.'

'Right,' I said.

She turned towards me and smiled and gave me a mini-hug and a kiss on the top of the head. 'Thanks for worrying about me, though. You're very sweet.'

I looked across the road and saw Barney giving me a huge wink and nudging Jenks. The two of them started giggling and I went scarlet.

Belinda looked over at Barney and Jenks and said, 'Boys. Honestly,' then diplomatically changed the subject by asking about Mum. So I told her about Mum's art class and how she could do really good pictures of the dog now. She asked about Dad and I said that he and I were virtually living in the shed these days on account of TJ. And, all in all, we had a very nice grown-up chat without any more hugging or ickiness at all.

Eventually Barney and Jenks finished filming and started packing up the equipment. Barney thanked Belinda again and apologized for having caused her a bit of a relationship problem. She told us not to worry and said she was quite looking forward to not spending any more weekends with a man who stored his dirty underpants on the floor and did the washing up at the end of the month. She also said that if we needed any more help we should just pop into the shop.

As we cycled away, Jenks and Barney started to tease me mercilessly about fancying Belinda. I decided to be mature and not rise to the bait. But by the time we reached the park I'd had enough. Unfortunately I was so busy yelling, 'I . . . Do . . . Not . . . Fancy . . . Her . . .' that I missed the gate completely and rode into a ditch. When I climbed out Barney and Jenks were standing, watching me with tears of laughter running down their faces. Barney was saying, 'That's what love does to you.' And I finally understood how Dad felt when TJ took the mickey out of his Rock 'n' Roll get-up.

I decided to cycle home on my own the long way.

I was almost there when I turned a corner and saw the unpleasant silhouettes of TJ and Fisty through the perspex back of the bus shelter by the laundrette. I pulled up out of sight and listened for a few minutes. TJ was telling Fisty all about the air rifle his dad owned, and how he used to go out and shoot squirrels when his parents weren't around. Fisty suggested that they go round to TJ's house and borrow the gun and got quite excited about this until TJ pointed out that the house was locked up. Fisty suggested they break in but TJ wasn't too keen on this idea so he changed the subject and started talking about this 'babe' he'd been chatting up who worked in the greengrocer's and how she obviously totally fancied him.

I doubled back and cycled round the block and approached the house from the other end of the street.

In the lounge, Elvis was singing *A-Wop-Bop-a-Loo-Bop-a-Wop-Bam-Boom* and Mum was painting a picture of Dad who was sitting on the sofa reading a book and complaining that he had pins and needles in his leg. But

Mum wouldn't let him move a muscle until she'd done his face.

I said, 'Hi,' went upstairs to my room, grabbed a copy of *Journey to the Bottom of the Marianas Trench*, came downstairs again, did a couple of waffles in the sandwich toaster, grabbed a glass of apple and blackberry squash and headed down the garden.

I marched into the shed, sat down on the sleeping bag, then immediately shot to my feet again, yelping and spilling my waffles and squash on account of a sudden shooting pain in my leg. I turned and looked down. There were two darts lying on my pillow and a third dangling from my jeans. I plucked it out, picked up the other two, turned round again and saw what Dad had hung from the back of the door.

It was my old dartboard. In the centre of the dartboard, slid underneath the dividing wires, was the photo of TJ with the tomatoes over his eyes and the slice of melon in his mouth. TJ's nose was now the bull's eye.

I brushed the sawdust and mud off the waffles, took a bite and got stuck into the first of 386 games.

By the time I'd finished TJ was riddled.

We had to wait another whole week before Barney finished editing the videotape and we were finally able to see the result of all our hard work. It seemed even longer to me because neither he nor Jenks had time to meet up outside school. Barney was too busy at what he called his 'mixing desk'. And Jenks was too busy building the 'Atomic Vaporizer', which was apparently vital for the film and about which he was being extremely secretive.

Me, I used Dad's powertools to make a frame for the dartboard, a large circle of green plywood onto which I glued red plywood letters reading DIE, TJ, DIE around the top and SO LONG, SCUMBAG round the bottom.

It seemed pathetically amusing at the time.

Of course when the three of us actually did get to meet up they gave me constant gyp about Belinda. I told them they were just jealous.

'It's OK,' said Barney. 'We understand. Love is a very beautiful and natural thing.'

'If you don't shut up I'm going to punch you.'

Etc., etc., etc.

Consequently it was a relief when we all went round to Barney's house on Saturday morning and closed the curtains and locked his mum out of the room and turned the video on for the first screening.

The film was stupendous.

It opened with a crashing, horror-film-style Yamaha organ chord from Aunt Jennifer and a large card reading THE INVASION OF THE KILLER BANANAS in bright orange poster-paint letters. Then other cards, reading, AGENT Z PRODUCTIONS . . . STARRING BELINDA HAZELMERE . . . DIRECTED BY BARNEY BERGMAN . . . PRODUCED BY BEN TARKOVSKY . . . BANANAS TRAINED BY JENKS B. DE MILLE.

'What's this B. De Mille stuff?' asked Jenks.

'Shut up,' shooshed Barney. 'I'll explain later.'

The screen went all staticky for half a second, then we saw Belinda loading crates of fruit into the back of the van. There were several close-ups of bananas, together with very significant-sounding electric organ chords. Then we saw Belinda get into the van and drive away.

The camera was wonky. There was crackle on the soundtrack and the picture of Belinda driving past the nuclear power station was the most unrealistic thing I'd ever seen on a TV screen. But, hey, it was post-modern, like Barney said, so that was all right. And, anyway, it soon hotted up when we cut to shots from *Meltdown!* – dials going into the red, men in white suits panicking, steam leaking through sealed metal hatches. Then there was an explosion and a huge mushroom cloud erupted into the sky. Belinda stared out of the van window in horror and everything started to bleach white. She gasped, covered her eyes and collapsed onto the wheel with her tongue hanging out.

It didn't matter that the van was driving through green countryside and the mushroom cloud was going up over the Nevada desert. It didn't matter that it was raining in one shot and sunny in the next. It was a film, a real film, and it was ours.

And when the sound of the explosion died down and the music slowed to a series of creepy, minor chords and the back door of the van swung open and the bananas began emerging, one by one, we knew that we had filmed the opening of a genuine cinematic masterpiece.

Fire Extinguishers, Neutrino Bombs and Chip Butties

I woke up the next morning feeling like the Ruler of the Universe on account of the fact that Barney, Jenks and I were obviously going to turn out to be internationally renowned film directors raking in the millions. Stuff TJ. Stuff Mrs Block. Stuff school. Stuff the Peasant's Revolt and ox-bow lakes and parallelograms. In five years' time we'd have servants and fun-jeeps and personal jets.

Even the sight of TJ's ugly snout ploughing his way through a bowl of Shreddies at the breakfast table didn't depress me. I waltzed into the kitchen whistling, 'Yes, We Have No Bananas', poured myself a bowl of Frosties, said, 'Good morning, Dearest Cousin,' and sat down to a brief encounter with Dr Scream before heading off to school.

TJ was rather thrown by my buoyant mood. He stared at me grumpily and was trying to work out something unpleasant to say when Mum came in with the post. She gave the bills to Dad and handed me the telegram from Talula, saying, 'Read that out while I do the bacon, will you, Ben? I'm running a bit late.'

I put Dr Scream down and picked up the telegram. 'Dear Trevor and Jane and Hello Ben. Stop. Weather is here. Stop. Wish you were lovely. Stop. Ha. Stop. Ha. Stop. Ha. Stop. A ship is on its way to rescue us. Stop. Not that we want to leave. Stop. It's one long party here. Stop. Yesterday this bloke got so drunk on the free champagne that he jumped off the diving board. Stop. But there was no water in the pool. Stop. Now he's dead. Stop. And they've put him in the fridge until the boat comes. Ha. Stop. Ha. Stop. Ha. Stop. Hope TJ is behaving himself. Stop. Fat chance. Stop. Tell him Harry will give him a thick ear if he's any trouble. Stop.'

Mum walked over and reached towards the telegram. 'Perhaps I should finish reading that on my own, Ben.'

'No,' said Dad, 'you carry on, Ben. I'm thoroughly enjoying it.'

TJ glared at Dad and me through narrowed eyes.

I carried on. 'It makes a nice change not having to listen to his dreadful music. Stop. And having to wash his filthy socks. Stop. If we're lucky the boat might sink before it gets here. Ha. Stop. Ha. Stop. Ha. Stop. Only joking. Stop. Send lots of love to my little darling. Stop. We will take him off your hands in a few weeks. Stop. Love and hugs. Stop. Trish. Stop. Kiss. Stop. Kiss. Stop. Kiss. Stop.'

I dropped the telegram beside my bowl and ate the last few spoonfuls of my Frosties. 'Great sense of humour, your mum,' I said to TJ. 'Got to run.' I grabbed a slice of toast, picked up my schoolbag and skedaddled.

Barney and Jenks woke up feeling like Kings of the Universe, too.

We spent the whole day pretending to be making a film called *School Wars – Agent Z Strikes Back*. At the beginning of every lesson, Barney rolled a piece of paper into a megaphone and spoke through it in a booming voice, saying, 'OK. Everyone quiet on set, please. *School Wars*. Scene 46a. Take 1. Action.'

Whenever one of us answered a question, one of the others filmed it with an imaginary mime-camera. At the end of every lesson, Barney picked up his megaphone again and said, 'Great, everybody. That's a rap.'

In the afternoon we had football, which Barney, Jenks and I did as a slow-motion sequence, so that we were constantly on the wrong side of the field moving at a tenth of the speed of everyone else. After fifteen minutes of this, Mr Salter gave all three of us a detention.

Barney pointed the imaginary film camera at him and said, 'Sorry, love. Can we do that one again? I need more anger, Mike. Give me anger, OK? That's beautiful.'

So Barney got two detentions.

We didn't care. We were having a great time.

After school we agreed to rendezvous at the Command Centre so we could discuss the next stage of the filming and Jenks could show us the work he'd been doing on the Atomic Vaporizer.

I went home, changed into my green combat trousers and the blue T-shirt Dad had bought me for Christmas which changed colour when it got warm so your armpits went pink. I made a quick dash to the shop to buy TJ a couple of cans of Pepsi Max (out of *my* money), grabbed Badger's lead, dragged him out of his basket and headed off to the park.

We were just passing the boating lake when we hit some serious flak from the laser bunkers on either side of the transdimensional portal into Sector Seven. I threw up the shields and slugged them with a couple of neutrino bombs for good measure. I hit the Chaos Generator, took a brief detour through parallel universe GX85, reversed the co-ordinates and re-entered normal space-time just in front of the portal at light-speed minus nine. We smashed through the Event Horizon, screamed onto the waste-ground and I gave it some truly smoking back-thrust to bring us to a halt before we ended up in Oslo.

I stuck the ship in PARK, took Badger's lead off, ran round the back of the Command Centre, slipped down into the cellar and ran upstairs to the lounge where Barney was sitting, waiting for Jenks and me to arrive.

'OK,' he said, without even asking for my Space Agency credentials, 'this is what we reckoned. You remember how we thought it would be really good to have TJ killed by the mutant killer bananas? Well, Jenks and I thought it would be even better if we got the chance to kill TJ ourselves.'

I slumped on the sofa, checked the oxygen content of the room's atmosphere, took off my helmet and gloves and started getting my breath back.

'So . . .' continued Barney, 'we have the bananas going round attacking people, like vampires do, turning them into yet more mutant killer bananas, which is how they take over the planet, by producing all these human-banana killer clones. And this is where Belinda's big bananas come in handy because the human-banana killer clones are, like, *huge*. And that's what happens to TJ. This banana attacks him and . . .'

'He turns into this mega-mutant banana vampire thing.'

'That's right,' said Barney. 'You film him doing his teeth and then going into the bedroom . . .'

'He doesn't do his teeth.'

'That's irrelevant, Ben. You film him going into his bedroom and turning out the light. Then, later, when he's not around, we film one of the original, small-sized, killer bananas creeping along the landing and chuckling in an evil way and opening the door of his bedroom and going inside. We hear the scream. Time passes. We see the sun coming up. An alarm goes off. The door of his bedroom opens and out comes TJ. Except it's not TJ. It's a mutant TJ-banana killer clone, which is you, wearing TJ's clothes, but with the top half of a big plastic banana sticking out of your collar over your head. And then . . .'

There was a loud clattering on the stairs. Seconds later the door was kicked open violently by Jenks, who was holding an enormous double-barrelled gizmo in his hands, pointing it at us and shouting, 'Eat atomic-fuelled death, yellow mutant banana scum!' And then, in a quieter voice, 'What do you think? Awesome, or what?'

It was awesome.

Jenks brought the Atomic Vaporizer over so we could examine it more closely. The body was made out of two old fire extinguishers painted purple. The nozzles of the extinguishers were masking-taped together on either side of a watering can spout, out of which a car aerial was poking. There was a kaleidoscope for a gun-sight and trigger stuck on underneath. Two defunct diving watches were glued to the side and the whole thing was covered in doodahs and gadgets and dials, just like you'd expect to find on a real live atomic vaporizer.

'Dad got the fire extinguishers from this office he's redecorating,' said Jenks, excitedly, 'because they're, like, out of date and they had to put new ones in. And he helped me weld it all together with his welding torch and he said I had to stand out of the way because it was really dangerous, and it *was* really dangerous because he set light to his shirt and I just grabbed his coffee and threw it all over him and he got really cross and I had to finish it off myself.'

'And then,' said Barney, turning to me and carrying on where we'd left off a few minutes back, 'we shoot these scenes of TJ – who's really you with your mutant banana head on – going round attacking people. And then we shoot a scene where the three of us see TJ and decide that we have to do something about him in order to save the human race. But TJ – who's really you – sees us and decides to catch us and bite our necks and turn us into mutant human-banana killer clones. He chases us into the Command Centre. And we shoot this part in two sections because you have to be you, and you also have to be TJ as well. So . . . we've barricaded ourselves into the Command Centre and the mutant TJ-banana clone monster is walking round outside trying to find an entrance. We charge up the Atomic Vaporizer, open a window and fire it at him. And the Atomic Vaporizer ray is a striplight I film separately and superimpose on the shot. And the vaporized TJ goes up in flames. But don't worry. It's not you inside the banana mask. We use a dummy. And when the dummy's on fire we see TJ's face superimposed on the flames at the last moment. And then we see TJ's trainers smoking on the ground in a little circle of ash and burnt grass.' He sat back with a great fat grin on his face. 'Sound good?'

'Yeah!' shouted Jenks. 'Eat atomic-fuelled death, mutant TJ scum! PZZZOWWW!'

'Damn good,' I said.

Barney took the camcorder out of his bag and handed it to me. 'OK, Captain. You know where the knobs are on this baby. Round 'em up and bring 'em home.'

'Oi! What are you playing at?' said TJ, who was slouched on the sofa, filling his face with Dad's last bag of gourmet hickory-smoked bacon crisps.

'I'm filming you,' I said.

'I can see that, you moron. Just cut it out, right?'

Mum gave him a weary scowl. 'TJ, couldn't you try to be just a *little* bit more pleasant.'

'No way!' he complained. 'You try having this twerp following you around all the time with his stupid camera.'

'I have done,' she said, flatly. 'He's been following me around for the last hour and it's really not that bad.'

'Yeah,' I explained. 'We're doing this project for school. It's like *What I did in the Holidays* except this is the twenty-first century and everything's really cyber and post-modern and kids can't write or read any more so we're doing videos instead of essays.'

'I give up,' said TJ, getting to his feet and stomping out of the room. 'God, I'll be glad when Mum and Dad get back and I don't have to live with you lot any more.'

When TJ had made his exit I turned to Mum and said,

'Brilliant. The whole living room to ourselves. See. I *can* be useful sometimes.'

She smiled at me and shook her head. 'Do you fancy having your portrait sketched?'

'It'll cost you,' I said.

So Mum drew me while I watched the second half of *Return of the Swamp Monster* and ate the chip butty and drank the milky coffee she'd made as my posing-fee.

Then we sat on the sofa together and watched *Dalston Junction*. Ronnie (whose real name was Mushtaq) was getting a right earful from his mum. At the age of twenty-nine, she was saying, it was high time he got married. So she and Mr Ahmed had got this nice Muslim girl lined up. All of which was rather depressing for Ronnie because he was in love with Sandra Coleman from the boutique who had curly blonde hair and freckles and wasn't really very Muslim at all, not even very Church of England actually.

After *Dalston Junction* I wandered down to the shed to play darts for a bit. At ten I came back up to the house and filmed TJ going down the landing and into the bathroom and coming out of the bathroom and going down the landing and into his bedroom, and got a whack round the head for my trouble. But it didn't matter because a cracking piece of video was in the bag and heading straight for Barney's mixing desk.

Back in the shed, I plonked the camcorder on Dad's workbench with the lens pointing through the window at the house then set the alarm for every fifteen minutes through the night and woke up each time and filmed a few seconds so Barney could link it all together and do a really good high-speed Time Passes section.

Understandably, I was a bit tired in the morning. I overslept, had to run to school with no breakfast, nodded off in Mrs Phelps' science class, snored loudly and rolled off the desk onto the floor when she prodded me with the board-rubber, and got a second detention to match Barney's.

Ulan Bator Is Not Far Enough

Sometimes, when your luck's in, the Big Scriptwriter in the Sky decides to give you a really easy ride for a few episodes. Our luck was in. We were getting an easy ride with knobs on. We were on a roll.

I was standing in front of the canteen hatch that lunchtime, queuing up for my beef slop and spotted dick, being congratulated by Barney and Jenks on my long night of heroic video-making, when we overheard TJ and Fisty talking a few places ahead of us.

Fisty was complaining that Breezeblock had confiscated his £300 ghetto-blaster. He was calling her some extremely rude names and vowing to get it back by any means possible. TJ, in turn, was complaining that Mr Lanchester had given him a detention for duffing up three kids who owned red fountain pens. Fisty suggested that the two of them meet up after school and go to the Grosvenor Centre to chat up babes and 'nick stuff'. TJ leapt at the chance, saying anything was better than spending another evening with 'the plonkers'.

The timing was perfect.

We headed back to my place straight after school. We cut the end off one of the large, plastic bananas and found that it fitted over my head perfectly. I got changed into TJ's pyjamas and spare trainers and put the banana-mask over my head. Then Barney borrowed a pair of bright yellow Marigold washing-up gloves from the kitchen cupboard to complete the costume. We recorded the sound of my alarm clock going off, then filmed me coming out of TJ's bedroom as a mutant killer banana clone, Frankenstein-style, with my arms stretched out in front of me, looking monsterish and growling, ready to take over Planet Earth.

Dad, who was feeling rather cheerful on account of TJ's absence, came upstairs in the middle of all this. He paused and looked at me dressed up as a banana and Barney holding a camcorder and said, 'How nice to have the house filled with normal children for a change.' And I think he meant it.

The sequence done, we packed up and headed over to Jenks' house, where we filmed me, dressed up as the mutant TJ-banana clone, attacking Jenks' younger sister, Brenda. We didn't tell her in advance that this was what we were going to do, and when I leapt out at her from the cupboard under the stairs, she screamed like a real

Hollywood star, fell over, spread her choc-ice up the wallpaper and passed out.

This looked so good that we then went out into the street and filmed me scaring members of the public. But the banana-mask didn't have eye-holes, and we decided to rap this particular scene when I accidentally stepped into the street and was hit by a cyclist.

Then we headed off to the Command Centre. We shot several minutes of me (playing the mutant TJ-banana clone) running through the trees, roaring and shouting, and another few minutes of Barney, Jenks and me (playing myself) running through the trees and looking over our shoulders as if we were being chased by a killer banana. We did some shots of me (playing the mutant TJ-banana clone) circling the park-keeper's cottage, banging the walls and rattling the windows, then some more shots of Barney, Jenks and me (playing myself) inside the building, looking terrified. We filmed Jenks charging up the Atomic Vaporizer and Barney pulling the boards off one of the windows. Then we filmed me (playing the mutant TJ-banana clone) staring up at the open window and Jenks pointing the twin-nozzles of the Atomic Vaporizer down at me, gritting his teeth and pressing the FIRE button.

I changed back into my own clothes. We filled TJ's pyjamas with rubbish and twigs and waste paper from the park bins, jammed the banana-head into the collar, rammed the Marigold gloves up the sleeves and stuffed the legs into the trainers. Then we stood the mutant scarecrow upright by attaching it to a big stick. We set light to it and filmed it burning down to a ring of ash surrounding one pair of smoking shoe-soles and three blistered fingers of a rubber glove.

That night, predictably, TJ kicked up a stink about his missing pyjamas and trainers. Mum said she was surprised he could find anything in the tip he'd made of my room. I said I'd tell him straight away if I happened to find them. Sir.

The following evening, we went round to Barney's house to help him film the striplight which was going to become the vaporizing ray. On the way home I bought Mum a new pair of Marigolds, telling her she must have dropped them into my schoolbag by mistake, though this didn't quite explain why they'd changed from Medium to Large. I suggested it might have been the poisonous atmosphere of old chewing gum and nose-pickings which had done something to the rubber.

On Wednesday evening we had to do our detentions. Luckily Potato-Head Dawson had drawn the short straw in the staff room that lunchtime. Potato-Head was a push-over. He didn't care what you got up to in detention so long as you kept quiet, stayed in your seat and didn't tell any of the other members of staff that he spent the whole two hours reading sci-fi novels behind his briefcase.

Well, that's what he usually did. This particular evening he remained awake long enough to do the attendance sheet (no TJ) then fell asleep for the following hundred and twenty minutes. So I got out Dr Scream's House of Horror, found the haunted fondue fork in the scullery, drove it into Dr Scream's heart to kill him, then made my way up his left nostril to look for his brain only to discover that YOU FOOL! DR SCREAM'S BRAIN DOES NOT EXIST. DR SCREAM DOES NOT EXIST. HE WAS JUST A BODY, A TOOL FOR THE AWESOME POWER OF THE DARK ONE . . . WHO WILL REMAIN BEYOND YOUR REACH FOR ALL ETERNITY . . . TO FIND OUT MORE BUY DSIG 2. £24.99 FROM ALL GOOD GAMES SUPPLIERS.

Barney spent his time writing out the end-of-film credits in felt-pen on pieces of large, white cardboard and Jenks discovered that it really is possible to eat four biros so long as you chop them up into very small pieces with your penknife first.

103

While Potato-Head was doing the attendance sheet, TJ was in Reggie's Veggies (so Belinda told me later), giving her a dose of his oily charm. She studiously ignored his advances for ten solid minutes, finally telling him she'd rather go out with a turnip because whilst a turnip looked exactly the same as him, a turnip would at least have some character. TJ winked, blew her a kiss, nicked a Granny Smith and swaggered out of the shop, straight into Mr Lanchester, who was popping into the florist's next door to buy something romantic for Mrs Lanchester.

Mr Lanchester asked him angrily why on earth he wasn't in detention. TJ said, 'Wind yer neck in, Bob,' and started laughing because he thought this was extremely funny. He bit into the Granny Smith and began walking away. Mr Lanchester grabbed hold of his collar. Buoyed up by Fisty's stories of his famous fight with Mr Lanchester last year, TJ thought he'd give it a go and took a swing at 'Bob'.

Mr Lanchester, however, had taken precautions since the embarrassment of last year's fight – a series of evening classes in self defence at the College of Further Education – and TJ found himself lying face-down on the pavement within seven picoseconds. Mr Lanchester gave him six detentions on the spot and promised to make a special arrangement to have them transferred to his original school when he went back.

On Friday night, Barney, Jenks and I filmed a few bridging sequences to connect the nuclear accident section to the TJ stuff – mutant killer bananas hiding behind garden walls, breaking in through people's windows, climbing secretly into the passenger doors of cars and, most importantly of all, slithering through our front gate, up to the door and in through the letter box.

Barney spent Saturday editing and mixing, and on Sunday the three of us sat down in Barney's lounge to watch the result.

The new stuff was stupendous. It really did look as if a mutant killer banana was following TJ into his bedroom and attacking him. The Time Passes shots of dawn coming up over our house which I'd done were really rather beautiful. And when I emerged from TJ's bedroom the following morning it was genuinely spooky. True, I was shorter than TJ and his pyjamas were a bit baggy on me. But the banana-mask and the Marigold gloves made it pretty convincing.

The chase scene was great, too. The scrappy changes between shots and the odd camera angles only made it seem more frenzied and frightening. When Jenks finally fired the Atomic Vaporizer at the mutant TJ-killer banana clone, the effect was brilliant. Even more so because Barney had recorded a screeching *PZZEEEYOW!!!* over the top of it. TJ caught fire and you couldn't see he was a dummy because the camera was shaking so much. TJ's ugly mug appeared in the flames just before he was completely vaporized, and when he was finally reduced to a pile of ash the three of us cheered fit to bust.

'Yeah. It's pretty good,' said Barney, casually. 'It'd be nice to add a few more scenes to flesh it out. Newsreaders on telly talking about the invasion. The army being mobilized. Crowds of bananas gathering up together to attack whole villages. That sort of thing. But we can do that later. I reckon we should release this as the commercial version of the film. We can do the Director's Cut later.'

Unfortunately, the Big Scriptwriter in the Sky is not unlike the scriptwriters on *Dalston Junction*. After they've given a character an easy ride for a few episodes they decide that the plot needs spicing up a bit. Like what happened to Danny with the gravel. Like what happened to Benny with the blowtorch. Like what happened to Barney and Jenks and me.

I should've realized what was happening when I came home on Sunday evening and walked into the kitchen to find Mum holding up a sodden brown-black sketchbook. There was a rather unpleasant mushroomy smell in the air.

'And what do you think this is, Ben?' she asked.

'Ooh,' I said, turning my head on one side. 'Train crash at night? In the modern style?'

Mum furrowed her brows at me. 'I found it under my mattress. Charcoal on its own would be bad enough. Mushroom soup on its own would be bad enough. But together . . .'

This, however, was only the first wee stormcloud arriving in advance of the tornado.

I trudged down the garden in disgrace, planning to read a little bit about the Marianas Trench until the guilt wore off. TJ was waiting for me in the shed. I had seen the light on and assumed it was Dad. I stepped inside and was hit in the shoulder by a dart. Not hard. Just a gentle lob. But it stuck in. And it hurt.

'Aaargh-ooch!' I yelped, pulling the dart out and massaging the wound. 'TJ, you berk, what are you playing . . . ?'

And then I saw it, dangling in TJ's hand. The dartboard. With DIE, TJ, DIE around the top and SO LONG, SCUMBAG round the bottom.

'A dart is the least of your problems,' he said, darkly.

The Breezeblock video . . . He was going to show everyone the video. I wanted to turn and run. But where to? London? Ulan Bator? Parallel universe GX85?

'Came in here looking for my pyjamas,' he said casually. 'Reckoned you probably had them, you being a little toe-rag. You know. Trying to get your own back on me behind my back, all sneaky like. And what do I find?' He got slowly to his feet and dropped the two remaining darts, one after the other, into the surface of the workbench. Thud. Thud. He walked around me to the door and turned and paused and said, casually, 'I'm going to turn your life into a living hell, Ben.'

Then he walked out into the darkness.

And the door banged ominously behind him.

Exit Mr Turnip

The sun was almost too hot. I rolled off the lilo into the warm, blue water and breaststroked slowly over to the swim-up bar where Finlay, my butler, was waiting for me. 'The usual, Sir?' he asked.

'That'll do nicely,' I said.

'One Tizer 'n' pineapple cocktail with a vanilla ice-cream float coming up,' he said, turning to take the ice-cream out of the swim-up fridge. 'Incidentally, Sir, you had a telegram from Belinda Hazelmere this morning. You remember, that rather charming film actress you met when we were at Cannes in May? She told me to tell you that her yacht will be anchoring in the bay in a couple of hours, and she wondered whether you might like to join her for some jet-skiing . . . Your drink, Sir.'

I sipped at my cocktail. 'Wire Belinda's yacht and tell her we'll get the launch ready after lunch and mosey on out.'

'That would be fine, Sir, except that you ARE A FOOL! BELINDA HAZELMERE DOES NOT EXIST. THE WHOLE OF THIS LUXURY COMPLEX DOES NOT EXIST. EVEN YOU DO NOT EXIST. YOU ARE SIMPLY A TOOL FOR THE AWESOME POWER OF THE DARK ONE . . . WHO WILL REMAIN BEYOND YOUR REACH FOR ALL ETERNITY. TO FIND OUT MORE BUY DISC 56. £4,500 FROM ALL GOOD FANTASY STOCKISTS.'

At this point Badger muzzled open the shed door, heaved himself onto the sleeping bag and woke me up with a single well-aimed blast of reeking dog-breath. I pushed him away and lay looking at the cobwebbed ceiling for some minutes. I didn't want to get up. Ever.

I didn't want to be alive. I wondered whether I could lie there and close my eyes and pretend to be dead for the next few years.

'Ben!' shouted Mum from the other end of the garden. 'Shift yourself or you won't get any sausages!'

I dragged my clothes on and wandered up the garden, Badger doddering at my heels. I went inside and trudged upstairs to the bathroom. There was no noise coming from TJ's room, which was odd since he usually stuck music on as soon as he woke up, just in case we forgot he was there. I paused and peered gingerly through the half-open door. Something was wrong. I pushed the door a little harder and it swung slowly back on its hinges.

No bombsite of clothes. No rucksack. No TJ.

I told myself not to get too excited. Maybe he'd just gone to school early. Maybe he was planning something with Fisty Morgan. Maybe . . . That was when I saw it. On the window sill. The video. *Breezeblock Comes a Cropper.* And beside it the photograph of Barney, Jenks and me sitting on the sofa in the Command Centre wearing our Z badges.

I couldn't believe my luck.

I grabbed the video and the photograph and high-tailed it downstairs, stopping briefly to grab a box of matches from the mantelpiece. I ran down the garden and threw the tape and the photo onto the remains of our last bonfire, covered it with dead leaves, poured a sprinkling of Dad's mower-fuel on top and set it alight.

'Should I ring for a doctor or is there a rational explanation for this?' asked Dad, appearing at my shoulder and handing me a bowl of Frosties and a cup of tea.

'TJ's gone.'

'Gone?'

'His clothes. His rucksack. His cassettes. Everything.'

'Ah.'

'This was the evidence.'

'Evidence of what?'

'You know, the blackmail thing.'

'Oh, right,' said Dad. 'So, he's just . . . like . . . vanished?'

'Yeah.' I could feel the relief beginning to spread through my body like the taste of a Tizer 'n' pineapple cocktail. I took a spoonful of Frosties.

'Well . . .' said Dad. 'I suppose I ought to be worried.'

'He's probably at Fisty's,' I said. 'Or maybe he's broken into his mum and dad's house . . .'

Dad looked up at the sky and let out a long, long sigh.

'Good, isn't it?' I said.

But it wasn't good. The Big Scriptwriter in the Sky hadn't finished with me yet. Or with Barney. Or with Jenks. Oh no. The Big Scriptwriter in the Sky was just warming up.

'Wow!' said Jenks. 'We really did vaporize him, then.'

'Video voodoo,' mumbled Barney, finishing off his own steak and kidney pie and moving on to Jenks'.

'The strange thing is . . .' I said. 'Last night, he was in the shed. He'd found this dartboard-thing that Dad made. It's got TJ's face on it. From a blown-up photograph. And

I made this frame that said DIE, TJ, DIE and SO LONG, SCUMBAG on it.'

'Cool,' said Jenks, unhelpfully.

I ignored him. 'And he threw a dart at me and said he was going to turn my life into a living hell. And I thought he was going to take the video into school and give it to Breezeblock. Along with the photo of us wearing our Z badges. Except, when I went into his room this morning . . . I mean *my* room . . . they were still there. So . . . I burnt them.'

'Quick thinking, Batman,' said Barney.

'Weird, though, isn't it?' I added.

'Don't look a gift horse in the mouth, that's my motto,' said Barney, moving on to the apricot crumble.

'What's a gift horse?' asked Jenks.

'It's an ancient Egyptian custom,' replied Barney without the tiniest flicker of a smile. 'They used to do up this horse in wrapping paper and post it to their enemies. And their enemies would unwrap it and give it the once-over. But when they opened the mouth there were these sharpened, metal spikes inside. On springs. And they'd shoot out and go straight through the enemy's forehead into his brain.'

'God, you do talk a load of twaddle,' said Jenks.

It was all Mum's fault. I mean, if she'd just breathed a sigh of relief, put her feet up and done nothing, it would all have turned out fine. But when there was no TJ at school, no TJ back home in the evening, no TJ in my room overnight and no TJ at breakfast she began to get twitchy.

112

So she rang Breezeblock to say that my darling cousin had gone AWOL, and Breezeblock made an announcement in assembly asking whether anyone knew where he was. No one had a clue.

Breezeblock notified the police and Mum, Dad and I were hauled into her office for a friendly chat with a Detective Inspector Hogmoor and a Sergeant Pickings.

The policemen asked if we had any idea where TJ might be and Mum said that he was probably staying with friends back home. Or maybe with that Morgan boy. She explained that TJ was a difficult and unpredictable young man and leaving without telling anyone where he was going seemed perfectly in character to her.

Mrs Block then turned and gave me some serious flak from the laser bunkers of her narrowed eyes. 'Ben,' she said, sharply, 'if you know of *anything* which could help the police in their enquiries . . .'

'There's nothing I can think of,' I said cheerily.

'Good,' she said. 'Good.' She stood up to signal the end of the meeting and said, 'Well, let's just hope this is a storm in a tea cup.'

It wasn't. Another day and TJ was still missing. The police grilled Fisty. They checked out TJ's parents' house. They quizzed the neighbours. They tracked down TJ's friends.

Zilch.

Three days after TJ vanished, I was lying on the sofa after school, eating one of our banana-extras and watching a documentary about climbing K2 without oxygen. The phone went, Mum answered it then walked into the lounge looking very dark indeed.

'That was Mrs Block,' she said.

I hit MUTE on the remote. 'What did she want?'

'Us. All three of us. In her office. Now, apparently.'

'I thought we'd been grilled, already.'

'So did I. But she didn't sound as if she was in the mood for a question and answer session.'

My guts churned like a washing machine full of wet cement.

'So get your shoes on and drag your dad up from the shed while I set the video for *Dalston Junction*. It's probably best if we get this thing over with as soon as possible.'

Twenty minutes later we found ourselves sitting round Breezeblock's desk in an atmosphere you could have used to strip paint.

Mum, who doesn't like being ordered about by anyone, especially when it involves missing *Dalston Junction*, said, rather frostily, 'So, Mrs Block, are you going to tell us what this is all about?'

In reply, Mrs Block leant down beside her desk, picked up my dartboard and dropped it onto her desk.

It had a photograph of TJ in the middle.

With 386 dart-holes in his head.

It had DIE, TJ, DIE written round the top in big, red letters.

It had SO LONG, SCUMBAG written round the bottom in big, red letters.

Dad squeaked weirdly and went a peculiar off-white colour.

The cement-filled washing machine in my stomach switched onto SPIN.

'Is this your dartboard, Ben?' asked Mrs Block.

'No,' I said. It seemed like the only sensible answer at the time.

Breezeblock spun the dartboard round. The words bEn SlmPSon were written across the back in my best, six-year-old handwriting.

'Er . . . I mean "Yes".'

There was a silence like the silence on the surface of the planet Pluto very early on a Sunday morning.

Then Mrs Block said, 'It was left in a parcel addressed to me outside the main doors of the school last night. Now, if I remember correctly, Ben . . . and I *always* remember correctly . . . you said you knew nothing which might help the police in their enquiries.'

'Nngh,' I said, because forming actual words was quite hard.

Mrs Block folded her arms over her large bosoms and glared at me. I wanted to pump a series of random digits into the Chaos Generator and scoot sideways out of reality. Sadly, however, the Chaos Generator DID NOT EXIST.

'A boy is missing,' said Mrs Block, with all the venom of a spitting cobra, 'a boy you wanted *dead*.'

'Oh, this is ridiculous,' said Mum. 'You don't seriously think that . . . ?'

'This is far from ridiculous,' hissed the headmistress.

'And I strongly suspect that the police will share my opinion.'

And then something quite extraordinary happened.

Just behind Mrs Block's head, TJ appeared at the window, grinning like an ape and waving at us. I thought at first that I was hallucinating, but I wasn't because Dad lifted his finger and pointed and shouted, 'Look! There he is! Out there!'

Mrs Block sat back in shock, then turned towards the window, but TJ had already sunk down below the lintel again. She turned slowly back to Dad and stared at him in angry, exasperated disbelief.

'It *was* him,' insisted Dad. 'He was there. Laughing. And waving. You saw him, Jane, didn't you?'

'Yes . . . No . . . I mean . . . I wasn't looking,' flapped Mum.

'Ben . . .' Dad implored me. 'You saw him, didn't you?'

'Er . . . yeah . . .' I said. 'He was there. Right outside the window.' I was still reeling from the shock. I sounded as mad as Dad.

'I'll get him,' spluttered Dad, leaping off his chair, spinning round, catching his toe on the rucked-up edge of the carpet, falling onto the doorhandle, wrestling it open and collapsing into the corridor.

Mrs Block and I and Mum stared at each other in silence for a few seconds. Then Dad appeared at the window, running backwards and forwards across the playground like a headless chicken looking for TJ.

'Your husband is quite clearly insane,' said Mrs Block.

116

'And judging by *this* . . .' she poked the dartboard as if it were a test-tube full of anthrax '. . . your son is equally deranged.'

Mum thrust her shoulders back, squared her jaw and shot from the hip. 'You will *not* talk about my family in this manner!'

'I have and I will,' retorted Mrs Block. 'And now, I must ask you to leave my office.'

Burning Rubber

We rounded up Dad and got into the car. The journey home was a touch tense on account of the fact that we had to explain to Mum why we'd done such a childish thing with the photograph of TJ. And things didn't improve a great deal when we pulled up behind a squad car and saw Detective Inspector Hogmoor and Sergeant Pickings waiting in our porch.

They were polite and cheerful. Clearly they hadn't heard about the dartboard yet. They asked if they could have a quiet word and Mum told them to step inside.

'We've decided to widen our search,' said Hogmoor, leaning against the mantelpiece and sipping at his mug of tea while Pickings and Badger played tug-of-war with a rubber bone. 'So, it would be useful if we could get our hands on a picture of this young lad.'

Mum, Dad and I looked at one another, not wanting to mention the photo in the middle of the dartboard. Though, to be honest, it wouldn't have helped anyone recognize TJ, what with the tomato-halves over his eyes and a slice of melon in his mouth, and the 386 holes in his head.

Then Mum had a brainwave.

'Ben?'

'What?'

'You took loads of pictures of TJ, didn't you? With that video camera.'

'Er . . .'

Mum smiled at the sergeant. 'It's his friend's. Barney's. He won it in some competition. Ben borrowed it one day and recorded everything in the house. Me, Trevor, TJ . . .'

'A video would be fine,' he said. 'We can take a still from it and circulate it round the station. Be a great help. So, Ben, have you got the tape?'

Having Breezeblock see the *Breezeblock Comes a Cropper* video would have been bad enough. Having the police watch a video of TJ being turned into a mutant killer banana and us burning him to death would make the Breezeblock video seem like a day at the seaside.

I was beginning to understand what TJ meant by 'living hell'.

'Well . . . ?' asked the sergeant.

'No. I haven't.'

'Well, someone must have it . . .'

'Yes . . . Right . . . It's . . .' I sounded like Murder Suspect Number One.

The two policemen narrowed their eyes at me, like they do in police series on the telly just before they say, 'We've got you bang to rights, Chummy.'

'It'll probably be at Barney's house,' said Mum, helpfully.

'And this Barney,' said Sergeant Pickings, taking out his notebook. 'Where does he live?'

Mum gave him the address.

The sergeant and his colleague put their hats back on. 'Well, thank you very much indeed for being so helpful. We'll pop over to see this young chap and take it from there.'

Mum saw them to the door and came back into the lounge. 'Ben?' she said. 'What's wrong with you?'

What was wrong with me? A heartbeat hovering around 700 bpm. Blood-pressure so high you could have used it to cook vegetables. A feeling in my guts like I was going through the transdimensional portal into Sector Seven at light-speed minus nine. And that was just for starters.

I ran to the window and waited till the squad car had pulled away. Then I broke the world indoor fifteen metres record getting out through the front door, leaving Mum standing in the middle of the lounge, looking at the smoking tyre-marks on the carpet. I leapt onto my bike and whipped it up to Mach 5 down the alleyway, did a handbrake turn into the park, covered two small boys in puddle-water, then headed for the exit to the High Street on the far side of the swings.

The police were travelling by car. They'd have to go via the dual carriageway. If I was lucky, if they caught enough red-lights or ran over a pedestrian accidentally or were hit by a meteorite, I could just about do it.

I blasted through the park-exit onto the pavement. The pavement was blocked by a suited businessman talking into his mobile phone. I scooted round him, catching his cuff on the end of my handlebar and removing his shirt and jacket in one effortless rip. I veered out into the traffic, narrowly avoided the front of a honking, screeching Transit van, and screamed headlong into Tranmere Crescent. I mounted the pavement at the end, went up the grass bank and sailed through the air over the low wall into the B & Q car park, slalomed between the trolleys full of two-by-four and plastic guttering and exited onto Fish Street.

Three roads left. Wimbourn Drive. Dexter Road. Oddson Road.

Barney's house.

No police car. I swooped into the driveway, hit the brakes, went over the handlebars, did a forward roll, banged the door with my head, thumbed the bell and panted like a steam train.

Barney's mum undid the latch. I shoved open the door and shot through into the hallway yelling, 'Barney! The videotape!'

He sauntered down the stairs, snacking leisurely from a bag of yoghurt-covered raisins. 'Ben,' he said, calmly. 'How can I help?'

'Video! Give me the video! Can't explain now! Police! Got seconds. Five. Ten. I don't know. Quick! Please!'

He crooked his finger at me. 'This way, my man.'

I pushed him into the lounge from behind, spilling yoghurt-covered raisins all over the carpet, then lunged towards the rack of videos.

'*Best of Noddy,*' he said.

'What!?'

'It's in the *Best of Noddy* box,' he said. 'Hidden.'

I grabbed the video and span round. Barney's mum was standing looking at me with her mouth hanging open, wavering slightly like she'd just drunk two pints of tequila straight off. I dodged round her, scooted down the hallway, out into the drive, onto my bike, out of the gate and straight over the bonnet of the squad car pulling up at the kerb.

When the stars cleared, I rolled over onto my back

and stared up into the bright, blue sky, most of which was being blocked by the upside-down silhouette of Sergeant Pickings.

'Haven't we met somewhere before, young man?' he asked, in that tone of voice policemen learn in Heavy Sarcasm class at training school.

He moved away and I got to my feet. He leant over the bonnet of his car and retrieved the video tape from where it had lodged under the windscreen wipers. 'Big Noddy fan, are we?'

Fruitcakes

We were summoned to the police station at the crack of dawn the following morning.

They were not the best circumstances for the first public showing of the film. We sat in an airless inter-view room with a locked door and a high barred window. Barney, Jenks and I faced Sergeant Pickings and Detective Inspector Hogmoor across a small wooden table. Mum and Dad sat in the corner, being the Responsible Adults.

In the opposite corner *The Invasion of the Killer Bananas* was playing on a video 'n' TV trolley.

It didn't come across quite the same on a second viewing. For one, it wasn't as funny. The two policemen didn't laugh at all. Neither did Mum. I heard a couple of snorty gargles from Dad but that was probably just nerves.

When Barney's neatly penned final credits had come to an end, Sergeant Pickings pressed STOP and Detective Inspector Hogmoor hit the START button of the tape machine on the table. 'Interview with Benjamin Simpson, Ian Jenkinson and Barney Hall,' he announced. 'Timed at 9.45 a.m. Thursday 10th April. Detective Inspector Hogmoor and Sergeant Pickings present. Also present, Jane and Trevor Simpson, parents of Ben.'

He tore open a sugar sachet and poured the contents into his styrofoam cup of coffee. 'OK, lads. Let's try and see this thing from my point of view. A kid goes missing. A kid . . .' he pointed to the dartboard which Mrs Block had thoughtfully delivered to the station'. . . whom you hated.'

'Er . . . about that dartboard,' said Dad.

'I'd prefer it if the boys spoke for themselves, Mr Simpson,' insisted Hogmoor.

I decided it was for the best if I didn't snitch on Dad for having made the dartboard. Mum was having a hard enough time already. If the two of us were under suspicion she would probably need major tranquillizers.

'We have this dartboard,' continued Hogmoor. 'We also have a videotape of the missing boy. A videotape which you, Ben, were very keen to keep hidden from us. On this videotape, which we have just witnessed, we see you three boys setting light to the missing boy and burning him alive. Now,' he sipped at his coffee, lingeringly, 'you tell me. What conclusions would you come to in my position?'

'Murder,' said Barney, who was keeping considerably more of his cool than either Jenks or I. 'Dead cert ten-stretch in The Scrubs by my reckoning.'

'Aha!' said Hogmoor victoriously. 'Who said anything about murder?'

'It was a joke,' replied Barney, wearily. 'Like the video.'

'Bit of a comedian, are we?' answered Hogmoor.

'I find it helps,' said Barney.

'Well, I find that jokes can be extremely revealing.' Hogmoor sipped at his coffee again and gave us a few seconds to digest this pearl of wisdom.

Out of the corner of my eye I could see Jenks hotching up and down on his seat, unable to contain himself any longer. 'You're so *stupid*,' he said, undiplomatically. 'Can't you see? It wasn't TJ. It was Ben. He was dressed up as a banana. He's shorter, see. And the clothes were all loose. And he had washing-up gloves on. And we did the shots separately. And it's called post-modern and mixing and it's what they do in Hollywood.'

Hogmoor sighed. 'Let's cut the garbage, shall we?' He stared at us, hard. 'Where's TJ?'

'Kuala Lumpur,' said Barney, straight off.

'Any more of your lip, Sonny,' snapped Hogmoor, 'and I'll have you for wasting police time. Is that clear?'

'Crystal,' said Barney.

'Now, maybe this will help to refresh your memories.' He leant down, picked up a thick cellophane bag from the floor and dumped it on the table. Inside were the charred soles of TJ's trainers, three blistered fingers of a Marigold washing-up glove and several pounds of ash.

126

'We found this . . . but, of course, you know where we found this, don't you? Ring any bells?'

'They're TJ's trainers,' I said. 'We nicked them for the film. Along with his pyjamas. I dressed up in them. Then we put them on this mutant banana scarecrow and burnt it and Barney put TJ's face on top of the flames in the video.'

'I am getting very tired of this,' said Hogmoor, though he looked like someone who would thoroughly enjoy grilling suspects from now till Kingdom Come. 'I am going to ask you one more time. And I don't think you need reminding that we may be talking about a very serious crime indeed, and that we are professionals. We shall find out the truth. That is our job. That is what we have been trained to do. And the longer you put off telling the truth, the more unpleasant it's going to be. So . . . Where is he?'

'Oh come on,' said Mum, from behind us. 'Of course they don't know where he is. Isn't that obvious?'

'You may think that your son is the nicest little boy in the world,' said Hogmoor. 'Most mothers do. We had a kid in here last week. Put nineteen stitches in another kid's head with a rake. His mother kept telling us how he bought her chocolates for her birthday and was nice to animals . . . I deal with some very sick minds, Mrs Simpson. The criminal mind *is* a sick mind. And where the criminal mind is concerned, *nothing* is obvious.' He turned back to Barney, Jenks and me. 'I shall ask you one final time. Where is he?'

No reply.

'Well,' said Hogmoor, 'I've wasted enough of my morning already. If you don't wish to co-operate that's fine. We have other methods. Mr and Mrs Simpson? I'd like you to make sure that all of these boys report to the police station once a day from now on. I don't want them doing anything silly. OK? Right. Interview terminated 10.10 a.m.' He hit STOP and ejected the cassette. 'Show them out, will you, Sergeant.'

The five of us clambered into the car and drove off.

'What on earth were you thinking of, making that ridiculous film?' asked Mum, crunching the gears aggressively.

Barney wisely refrained from the usual wise-crack reply and the question hung in the air for several seconds. Dad, however, hates uncomfortable silences and invariably ends them with some totally inappropriate comment. 'Oh, I don't know,' he said cheerfully. 'I thought it was quite good, really.'

'Good?!' snapped Mum. '*Good?!* Ben has just been grilled by the police who think he's done away with his cousin. I have been grilled by that Block woman who thinks I'm the world's worst mother. And now we have to take Ben to the police station every day because they think he's going to try and flee the country. You call that *good*?!'

'But TJ's *not* dead, is he? Or kidnapped. I saw him. Out of Block's window.'

'Did you?' asked Mum, shooting a red light with no reduction in speed whatsoever. 'Trevor, sometimes I wonder who's got the smaller mental age, you or Ben, I really do. Making that dartboard. Running round that playground like some demented greyhound. I wouldn't be surprised if you helped them make that idiotic video.'

'Now hang on a minute!' protested Dad.

'Brainless moron!' shouted Mum as she swerved round a wobbly cyclist outside the Taj Mahal Takeaway.

'Look,' said Dad, trying hard not to look out of the windscreen. 'Sooner or later TJ will turn up. And then everything will be fine.'

Dad was right. TJ would turn up. He was out there somewhere. He'd get bored. His underwear would start to smell. He'd miss the chocolate Hob-Nobs. Everything really would be fine.

I leant over to Barney and whispered, 'It's like we've gone through this hole in the reality continuum and we're actually living in *Dalston Junction*.'

'Honestly, Ben,' tutted Barney, 'you do watch some rubbish.'

At which point the car zig-zagged sickeningly as Mum twisted round in her seat. 'And *you* can be quiet. The lot of you. I've already had more than I can take of your so-called humour.'

'It's not Ben's fault,' complained Dad.

This was the last straw.

The car mounted the pavement outside the school gates and screeched to a halt.

'Out!' said Mum. 'All of you! And Ben . . . You are going to behave like an angel for the rest of today. If you

129

give Mrs Block any . . . and I mean *any* . . . cause for complaint, I will personally wring your neck.'

We clambered out of the car.

Two seconds later, Mrs Block burst from the main doors like a guided missile and strode across the playground towards us.

Mum got out of the car ready for a showdown.

Mrs Block told Mum that she didn't want the three of us in her school creating a bad influence whilst we were under investigation for a serious criminal offence. Mum told Mrs Block that she didn't want her son being educated in a school run by such a narrow-minded, dictatorial old bat. Dad sank down into the passenger seat and entertained himself by fiddling with the radio-cassette, which suddenly blared out 'I've got a lovely bunch of coconuts', just as Mum was delivering her riposte.

Mrs Block turned and stormed off and Barney said to Mum, 'You were brilliant, Mrs Simpson.' Mum swivelled round, smacked Barney on the side of the head with a juddering *Thwock!* and ordered us back into the car.

By six o'clock TJ had made the local news.

'Thomas Bagnell, also known as "TJ" went missing several days ago,' said the newsreader, as a shot of TJ from our video appeared on the screen (my darling cousin stretched on the sofa, filling his face with Dad's gourmet hickory-smoked bacon crisps). 'Foul play is suspected and three local boys have been questioned by the police. No body has been found, however, in spite of a widespread search by fifty officers . . .'

'So *that's* where my crisps went,' said Dad.

Mum glared at him.

In some ways, being under suspicion for first degree murder was rather good. No isosceles triangles, no Wars of the Roses, no *Bonjour, je m'appelle Ben*.

On the other hand it did have its drawbacks. Ordinarily, with so much time on our hands, we'd have made a radio-controlled shark fin and sailed it round the boating lake. Or jammed a couple of old shoes under the edge of a skip with the toes poking out and run round shouting, 'Help, help! It fell on top of him!' Or kidnapped garden gnomes and ransomed them for king-size bars of Cadbury's Fruit and Nut. That kind of stuff.

But that kind of stuff seemed unwise in the present circumstances. Ditto using the camcorder. Not to mention the fact that the police had been sniffing round the Command Centre . . .

As a result we had plenty of time to think about TJ joining the Foreign Legion under an assumed name and never coming back. About him being holed up in an empty house somewhere and having some horrible accident entirely of his own devising. About Harry and Trish coming home and finding out what had happened and Harry sending the lads round to administer justice in some darkened alleyway.

Barney's parents were not over-sympathetic. They took the view that Barney had made his own bed and had to lie in it. Jenks' parents were not much better. Julie had put someone in hospital only last year after an argument about her drumming at a Thrashfist gig. And his dad had done a month in the nick after selling a Ford Escort he'd welded together from two entirely different halves of crashed Ford Escorts which then unwelded themselves in the fast lane of the M65, almost killing a chicken farmer from Norwich. So, in their eyes, it wasn't *completely* beyond question that their son had murdered TJ.

Only Mum and Dad really stood up for us. True, relationships were strained a little by Dad having to lie about where TJ was every time Trish rang up from the Hotel Countryclub ('Trish . . . ? Trish . . . ? I can't hear you . . . I think the phone must be on the blink.') But they knew we weren't homicidal killers.

On Day 6 of the Strange Case of the Vanishing Human Banana, Barney, Jenks and I were summoned to the police station for our second interview. We geared ourselves up for another grilling but were rather taken aback when Mum was told to wait in reception and we were ushered into a small room with comfy armchairs to be greeted by a bearded man with a woolly cardigan and a notebook who said, 'Come in and sit yourselves down. My name is Mr Gravely. You can call me Michael. I'm a doctor.'

Barney said, 'Oh, that's lucky. I've got this strange rash on my bum.'

Dr Gravely didn't laugh. He just jotted something down in his notebook and said, 'No, not that sort of doctor. I'm a psychiatrist.'

'Are you going to put us in the funny farm?' gulped Jenks, a note of genuine panic in his voice.

'I just want to have a little chat with you, that's all,' he said, smiling.

'What do you fancy?' said Barney. 'Football? The weather? Quantum theory?'

Dr Gravely jotted something else down in his notebook. 'I would like to talk to you about Ben's cousin, TJ.'

'Are you going to give us a truth drug?' asked Jenks.

Dr Gravely rubbed his forehead. This was proving harder work than he'd expected. 'OK,' he said, 'let's begin at the beginning. I'd like each of you to spend ten minutes telling me all about your home life, your childhood, your school, your hobbies, your parents . . . Do you think you could do that for me? Jenks . . . would you like to kick off?'

If I was Jenks and I'd wanted to give Dr Gravely the impression that I was a normal, well-adjusted, law-abiding kid I probably wouldn't have told him about Kevin bringing his bed through the lounge ceiling playing trampolines. Or Julie riding her motorbike through the Grosvenor Centre stark naked. Or losing Wayne in a dumper truck on the M42. But I guess Jenks thought these were the kind of things that all normal, well-adjusted families did.

By the time he'd finished, Dr Gravely had clearly decided we were all loonies, so Barney went for broke and indulged his creative side. He told Dr Gravely that he was the secret love-child of a model and a famous MP.

He had been brought up by his aunt and her husband. And they were very nice. OK, so his uncle drank too much and his aunt had a bit of a shoplifting problem. But they went on long holidays without him, which meant he could have wild parties all the time.

Clearly, Barney had seen far more of *Dalston Junction* than he cared to admit.

Me, I thought what the hell, we were in this together, so I told Dr Gravely all about my friend, Mortimer, the large, pink crocodile who lived on the moon and came down to earth using the matter-transport system in my wardrobe to sit on the old armchair in my bedroom, drink Tizer 'n' pineapple cocktails and chat with me when my other friends weren't around.

Dr Gravely used up quite a lot of his notebook and ran an entire biro dry.

'Wonderful,' he said, 'Now, why don't we, erm . . . talk about this film of yours . . . *The Invasion of the Killer Bananas*? Tell me a little bit about that.'

'It's a documentary,' explained Barney. 'We had to make it. We knew that if we didn't make it, then no one would believe us. You see, they want to take over the planet. And they're *going* to take over the planet if no one stops them. They're out there now. Even as we speak. Gathering together on pieces of wasteland and behind shrubberies. Plotting with one another. Sharing information.'

'And "they" are . . . ?' said Dr Gravely.

'The Mutant Killer Banana Clones,' explained Barney. 'Except you probably won't have seen them. They're cunning. They have to be cunning to have got this far. And even if you did see them, there's nothing you could do. You have to have an Atomic Vaporizer.'

'Right . . . I see . . .' said Dr Gravely, scribbling madly. 'And this . . . Atomic Vaporizer . . . this is the weapon with which you . . . "vaporized" . . . Ben's cousin?'

'That's right,' said Jenks, 'PPZZZZEEE-OWWW!'

'So, erm, now he's . . . dead?'

'Vaporized,' said Jenks. 'Totally vaporized.'

'Everyone *thinks* he's dead,' I explained carefully. 'But the Atomic Vaporizer doesn't kill you. It just destroys your atomic structure in this particular sector of reality. Then it restructures your molecules in a different sector.'

Dr Gravely nodded and smiled, as if we really were

135

talking about football, or the weather, or quantum theory. 'Which means that he is . . . where, exactly?'

'Sector Seven,' I said.

'And how does one get to this . . . "Sector Seven"?'

'You hit the transdimensional interface doing something just under light-speed. Then *Whammo!* Straight through the Event Horizon.'

'Mmm,' hummed Dr Gravely. 'Not an easy journey, then.'

'Not too bad,' I said. 'You might have to take a microdetour through one of the parallel universes in the GX band if the flak's really steaming. So you'll probably need a Chaos Generator. Just in case.'

Dr Gravely's head went down and he began scribbling madly again. Barney turned to me and winked.

Dr Gravely looked up. He'd run out of notebook. 'Well, I think that's enough for today, boys. It's been . . . extremely informative. Thank you very much indeed for being so forthcoming. And now . . .' He stood up.

'Hang on,' said Barney, a sudden note of panic in his voice. 'We must give you the blueprints for the Atomic Vaporizer. Now that you know about the Mutant Killer Bananas. It's not safe out there.'

He looked at us, smiled very calmly, glanced over his shoulder to make sure that no one else was listening and said, under his breath, 'It's all right. I've already got one. So don't you worry about me . . . And now I think we should all go and find Mrs Simpson.'

Foam Fest

'OK, bring it in, Sergeant,' shouted Detective Inspector Hogmoor.

The door of the interview room opened and in came Pickings, carrying the Atomic Vaporizer which he dropped onto the desk in front of us with a loud *Donk*!

Hogmoor leant closer to the tape machine. 'Sergeant Pickings enters the room carrying item 4b found at the derelict park-keepers' cottage yesterday . . .'

'Thank goodness! You've got it,' said Barney. 'I thought it might have got lost. Then there would've been no hope whatsoever for the human race.'

'SHUT! UP!' shouted the detective inspector. 'Now . . .' He took several deep breaths to calm himself down. 'Yesterday afternoon I spoke to Dr Gravely, the psychiatrist. He seems to think that you are completely crazy. He seems to think that you believe the world is being overtaken by bananas.' His voice was getting louder and louder. 'He seems to think that you believe Ben's cousin was some kind of alien who had to be destroyed. He seems to think that you believe this . . . this pile of junk is some kind of laser weapon for sending people into another universe.' He got to his feet and leant forward across the table and roared, 'I'LL GIVE YOU "BANANAS"!'

'Now, steady on . . .' said Dad, who was sitting in the corner being the Responsible Adult present this morning.

'You can shut up, too!' grunted Hogmoor. 'My patience is beginning to wear extremely thin.' He sat down again. 'Now, let me tell you something. I don't go in for all this psychobabble gimcrackery. Some of those so-called psychiatrists are crazier than the people they lock up. So you listen to me and you listen hard. You might be able to pull the wool over Dr Gravely's eyes but you can't pull the wool over mine.' He banged his hand on the table.

At which point, Barney, for some twisted, suicidal reason, decided to stick his neck out just about as far as it would go.

'Be careful,' he said.

'WHAT?!'

'The Atomic Vaporizer,' explained Barney. 'It has a very delicate trigger mechanism.'

'AAARGH!' bellowed the detective inspector, clearly approaching an end-of-tether state of mind. 'THERE IS

138

NO TRIGGER MECHANISM! THIS IS NOT AN ATOMIC VAPORIZER!' I was tempted to ask whether he'd been involved in writing the text for Dr Scream's House of Horror but it did not seem like the most appropriate moment. 'THIS . . .' He slowly got a grip on himself. 'This . . . is just a pile of scrap metal welded together and painted purple. Look . . .'

'No!' screeched Barney. 'Not the FIRE button!'

'IT IS NOT A FIRE BUTTON!' bellowed Hogmoor, losing control once more.

But it was, quite obviously, the FIRE button. It had 'FIRE' painted in red just above it. And the detective inspector pressed it.

What happened next was perhaps the most unexpected event of the previous eventful three weeks. I don't think even Jenks would have put money on it. The extinguishers might have been past their sell-by date but they could have put out a blazing oil-refinery judging by their performance.

There was a deafening *FFFFSSSS!!!* and 200 gallons of foam erupted from the twin nozzles, travelling at something very near light-speed. The spray hit Pickings in the chest, knocking him backwards off his chair onto the floor, taking Hogmoor with him. The Atomic Vaporizer started spinning like a Catherine Wheel with the force of the blast, whirled off the table and began ricocheting around the floor, pumping foam and giving Jenks a meaty gash on the ankle. Two seconds later we were all covered in the stuff. Five seconds later the room was thigh-deep in foam, a huge spout exploding from beneath the surface every now and then as the extinguisher nozzles swivelled ceiling-wards before dipping again. The six of us were slipping and stumbling, desperately trying to avoid the thirty kilos of hyperactive scrap metal thrashing around our feet. Fifteen seconds later the foam was up to our chests. Pickings reached the door and dragged it open against the growing pressure of the foam and fell into the corridor, surfing a gargantuan wave of white froth towards the reception area. Twenty seconds later the extinguishers finally ran dry.

We listened to the Vaporizer spinning slowly to a halt somewhere underneath the whipped-cream waves as they slowly began to ebb away through the door.

And then there was silence.

Barney waded over to the middle of the room and

scooped out a few cubic metres of foam so that the tape machine on the table was visible once more. He leant down close to it and said, '11.27 a.m. Detective Inspector Hogmoor pressed the FIRE button on item 4b, the Atomic Vaporizer. He has now been vaporized. Any correspondence intended for him should now be forwarded to Sector Seven, just past the transdimensional interface. Interview suspended.'

'GET OUT!' yelled a submerged Detective Inspector Hogmoor from somewhere near the floor in the far corner of the room. 'GET OUT! *JUST GET OUT OF HERE!*'

'Oh, deary, deary, me,' said Dad, pulling up at the kerb outside the house and wiping the tears from his eyes. 'I have never . . . never in my entire . . .' He was still laughing. 'In my entire life . . . seen anything . . . quite so funny.'

He took his seatbelt off and went to open the door. 'OK, Ben. Let's get a grip on ourselves.'

'Probably best,' I said.

'Telling your mother is going to have to be a master-piece of diplomacy.'

'We're done for, then.'

'I think,' he said, 'I think not laughing might be a good first step.'

'Sure.'

'Here goes, then.'

We put on straight faces, got out of the car and squelched our way to the front door, dripping foam-gobbets up the path. Dad put the key in the lock and we stepped inside.

'Might be best if we got our wet clothes off here,' said Dad.

The phone rang and I leant over to pick it up, trying not to drip into the wellington rack.

'Hullo? Two-four-six, zero-two-two.'

I heard the *meep-meep-meep* of a phone box waiting for money to be shoved in, then a voice. 'Ben!' said TJ. 'Got you at last! How are you doing, me old mate?'

I turned to see Mum appearing at the other end of the hall, saying, 'Ben! Trevor! What in the name of . . . ?'

'Just thought I'd give my favourite cousin a ring,' said TJ. 'How did you like the dartboard stunt? Pretty good, eh. You see, I can think up some fairly wicked practical jokes myself when I put my mind to it. Bet you and Mrs Block had a good old laugh about that one . . . Cat got your tongue, Ben? Or have you lost your sense of humour? Oh well . . . Hope your folks aren't missing me too much. Can't say I'm missing them.'

'Where are you?'

TJ laughed. 'You must think I'm brain-dead. You really must. You reckon I'm going to tell you where I am so you can pop round and get your own back? You silly, silly boy. Well, got to run. Hope life's not too boring without me. Cheerio.'

The phone went dead.

'Well,' said Mum, 'are you going to tell me why you're both sopping wet, or not?'

'It's a long story,' said Dad.

'That was TJ,' I said.

The wet carpet suddenly became irrelevant.

'Well, where on earth is he?' asked Mum.

'He wouldn't say. He was in a payphone.'

A lightbulb went on above Dad's head. '1471,' he said. 'Ring 1471.'

I rang 1471.

'Telephone number. Oh. One. Eight. Six. Five,' said the robot-voice. 'Eight. Seven. Nine. Nine. Two. Three. Called at. Twelve. Forty-two. Hours. Today. To return the call press 3.'

I grabbed the pad and wrote the number down.

'We should ring the police,' said Mum. 'Give them the number. Tell them he called. Tell them he's alive and well.'

'Sure,' snorted Dad, sarcastically, 'like I told Mrs Block that he was standing outside the window of her office.'

'Trevor,' complained Mum, 'you're dripping *everywhere*. Get into the kitchen. And take those clothes off. You too, Ben.'

I peeled the top sheet from the phonepad and wedged it under the phone then wandered into the kitchen to remove my trousers.

A couple of minutes later, while Dad loaded the washer-dryer and tried to fob Mum off with some ridiculous story about a pipe bursting in the police station, I slipped back into the hall and rang Jenks and Barney and told them to come over as quickly as possible.

'But I'm grounded,' said Barney: 'As of about three minutes ago, when I wandered in covered in foam.'

'Well, escape,' I insisted. 'It's TJ. He rang. From a call box. I've got the number. And it's local. So bring that Ordnance Survey map of the town your dad's got.'

'I'm shinning down the drainpipe now,' said Barney, and hung up.

They arrived in ten minutes. Barney had changed into dry clothes. Jenks, on the other hand, was still dripping foam on account of his sister Cheryl having broken the front door key off in the lock and the whole family being on the lawn. So I lent him a pair of shorts and my I♥NY T-shirt and we went into my room for an emergency conference.

Barney unfolded the map and spread it on the floor. 'Right. A public phone box . . . Jeez, Ben, there are millions of them.'

'There was traffic noise in the background, so he was near a biggish road,' I said.

Barney examined the map. 'Well that cuts it down to about three hundred.'

'The tent!' I said. 'He's got the tent! You know, from his holiday in the Lake District. It was in his rucksack. He'll be camping.'

'Or not,' said Barney. 'He could be anywhere. Someone's garage. An old factory . . .'

'Which is exactly where they'd be looking. Except they haven't found him, have they? And they don't know about the tent. So he must be camping, right? And he must be camping somewhere pretty tucked away or someone would've spotted him, right?'

144

'OK,' said Barney. 'Phone boxes on big roads near woods and copses . . .'

We gathered round the map and went over it with a fine-tooth comb. We narrowed it down to sixteen phone boxes. It was a long-shot, but it was worth it. Get to him before anyone else did and we could summon up the truly awesome power of Agent Z to give him a homecoming he'd never forget for the rest of his life.

We headed downstairs and out of the front door to rev up the bikes.

'Where are you lot off to?' asked Mum, suspiciously.

'Ah . . . to . . . er . . . look for TJ.'

'I thought you didn't know where he was.' She walked up to me and tried to stare into my brain with those special X-ray eyes that mums have. 'Is there something you haven't told me, Ben?'

Barney came to my rescue. 'He was in a phone box, Mrs Simpson. And Ben heard this ice-cream van passing, playing *Nessun Dorma*. It's the theme tune for the Gallone vans, so we're off to the depot to see if we can check out their route map.'

'I'll go and ring the police and tell them,' said Mum. 'And you lot . . . If you so much as . . .'

'We'll be angels,' I said.

Mum turned and went inside.

'Nice one,' I said to Barney.

We hit the road.

The Grand Plan

We hit gold with phone box number fourteen.

'879 923!' Jenks yelled. 'This is the one.'

Barney turned and pointed towards Helmsdon Wood. 'So, he's in there somewhere. Men, we have our quarry in range. Let's lower our visibility potential and get serious about this.'

We retreated to the rear of a nearby bus shelter and Barney took the map out of his bag. 'OK. We lock up the bikes here.' He jabbed the map with his forefinger. 'Near the bridge. Then we sweep the area . . .' he licked his finger and held it up in the air '. . . from this direction. Upwind.'

'Come on,' I scoffed. 'He's not going to *smell* us.'

'We have to take every possible precaution, Ben. No sudden movements. No talking . . .'

FLRGBRGL! went Jenks' stomach.

'And none of that if you can possibly help it.'

'Sorry,' said Jenks. 'Dad did the breakfast this morning. Had to scrape this furry stuff off the bacon.'

'We have to slip through those trees like jungle cats,' continued Barney, ignoring Jenks. 'We go in. We sight the target. We move out. Quick. Clean. Efficient.'

'Yes sirree, Captain,' I said, slipping into my US fighter-pilot voice, 'let's check the fuel pressure and load up the bomb hatches and . . .'

Barney turned to me. 'No funny stuff, Ben. This is business.'

We cycled to the bridge, dumped the bikes and entered the wood. Fifty metres in and the undergrowth began to thicken. Nettles. Thorns. Mud. We were on our stomachs now, inching forward. Barney tapped me on the shoulder. I turned.

'There,' he whispered. 'Look.'

I moved forward a few centimetres and stared between the leaves. Twenty metres away, in a hollowed-out clearing of bracken and branches. A tent. A pile of tin cans. A pair of boots. A half-empty packet of chocolate Hob-Nobs.

'Right, let's kill him,' whispered Jenks. 'Let's really kill him. Totally.'

'Shut up, you prat!' hissed Barney.

'Oh yeah, right,' said Jenks. 'Sorry.'

Barney excavated a small stone from the earth beneath his chin, took aim and thumb-flicked it up through the foliage. It flapped and pattered through the

leaves and came down on the side of the tent with a distant *Ftup!*

We waited.

Three seconds later, TJ's head appeared in the doorway. He looked around, squirmed out and got to his feet with an open can of Pepsi Max in his hands. He looked around again, shrugged, sat down, ate a Hob-Nob, lit a cigarette and stared straight at the bracken where we were lying.

We froze. TJ stared. Jenks' stomach went *FRGL!* We held our breaths. TJ yawned and scratched his bum. He finished off the Pepsi Max, chucked the can onto the canpile, leant into the tent, retrieved a magazine and began reading. The magazine was called *VROOM!* On the cover a woman in a bikini was lying along an enormous motorbike. She didn't look very comfortable.

Three minutes. Four minutes. TJ finally stubbed out his cigarette, turned round, threw the magazine through the tent-opening and crawled inside.

We began slowly making our way back through the undergrowth towards the edge of the wood.

'Any luck?' asked Mum.

'Pardon?' I said.

'The ice-cream van route,' she said.

'Nothing I'm afraid,' said Barney. 'The drivers are all freelance. Go where they want, kind of thing. And anyway, the Mr Scoopy vans have started using *Nessun Dorma*, too. Bit of a wild goose chase, really.'

'Well, that makes two of us,' said Mum, wearily. 'I rang the police station and all I got was an earful from some desk sergeant. Said the kind of help he got from my family was the kind of help he could do without. Goodness only knows what that was all about.'

'Incidentally, Mrs Simpson,' said Barney, 'you haven't got any of your delicious home-made coffee cake lying around, have you? What with it being lunchtime and us having cycled all over the town? I gave my mum the recipe, but she never gets it *quite* right.'

'Honestly. You could smarm for England,' said Mum, opening the cupboard. 'Now, if you could try and restrain yourself from finishing the whole thing in one sitting . . .'

'For you, Mrs Simpson, anything.'

'Don't push your luck,' said Mum.

*

Post-snack, we headed back upstairs to plot revenge.

'I know,' said Jenks, 'why don't we, like, sneak up on him at night and knock him unconscious and dress him up in women's clothes and high-heels and stuff and then handcuff him to the railings opposite the police station so they find him there in the morning?'

'Because we'd be done for GBH,' said Barney. 'Because the police station is open all night, strangely enough, so we'd be seen. And because you can't ride a bike carrying an unconscious body on the parcel rack. Here.' He picked up Dr Scream's House of Horror and chucked it to Jenks. 'Shut up and play with this. Now, Ben . . . We've got to try and get TJ into some serious trouble, right.'

'Except that he *will* be in trouble when they find him.'

'For what?' said Barney. 'For running away? I mean *serious* trouble. Not just a ticking off from your mum and a rap over the knuckles from the police.'

'Hey,' said Jenks, 'how do you get through the front door?'

'Zap the knocker,' I said. 'The big, black skull in the middle of the door.'

Barney flopped back onto the bed and closed his eyes. 'OK,' he said, 'lateral thinking,' and pressed his fingers to the side of his head.

'What's "lateral thinking"?' asked Jenks, absentmindedly.

'Not having you disturbing me,' said Barney and lapsed into silence.

I gave up. Barney would get there first. He always did. Trying to compete wasn't worth it. I picked up my copy of *Natural Born Killers: Murder in the Animal Kingdom* and read all about how the female digger wasp lays her eggs inside a caterpillar and stings it so that it can't move and the baby wasps can eat it alive from the inside.

Finally, Barney sat up and said, 'Do you reckon TJ and Fisty are in touch with each other?'

'I don't know,' I replied. 'Is it important?'

'It could very well be.'

'Well I suppose we could find out. You know, get his number out of the phone book and ring up pretending to be TJ. If you can do a decent impression. See what he says . . .'

We headed downstairs and looked up the Morgans' number in the phonebook. Barney rang up and asked for Fisty. Fisty materialized at the other end of the line. 'It's TJ,' said Barney in his TJ-voice, keeping it simple.

'Hey! Mate!' said Fisty. 'Long time no hear. What're you doing, man? You know the fuzz are looking for you . . . ?'

'I'm sorry,' said Barney, switching to a squeaky, secretarial whine, 'you'll have to ring off. This line is reserved for human beings.' He put the phone down and turned to me. 'Right . . .'

'What are you lot up to?' said Mum, crossing the hallway with a paintbrush in her mouth and a mug of coffee in her hand.

'Ringing the Mr Scoopy depot,' said Barney. 'No luck, though. All their drivers are freelance, too.'

'Fact One:' said Barney, 'Breezeblock confiscated Fisty's ghetto-blaster. Fact Two: he said he was going to get it

151

back. Fact Three: TJ was bragging to Fisty about his dad's air rifle.'

'So . . . ?'

'So we meet up with TJ at his hide-out. We tell him we know everything. How he and Fisty broke into Breezeblock's house to get the ghetto-blaster back. How they used TJ's dad's air rifle. How there was a scuffle and Breezeblock ended up in hospital. We tell him the police have already arrested Fisty.'

'But none of this happened,' I said.

'Quite,' said Barney, smugly. 'So, from where TJ's sitting, it looks as if Fisty nicked Harry's air rifle then broke into Breezeblock's house on his own. Then told the police that TJ helped him do it. Remember, the gun will be covered in TJ's fingerprints from all that squirrel-shooting.'

'He is *never* going to believe all this twaddle,' I protested.

'So we ring the police. We tell them we've seen a bald teenager trying to break into the Bagnells' house. We take TJ over there. The police turn up to sniff around. TJ sees them and realizes something's up.'

'And even if he does believe it,' I said, 'he'll just scarper.'

'And we'll help him,' said Barney, 'Tell him your Uncle Bernie's going to put him up for a few weeks in Aberdeen. Tell him your dad's going to drive him to the station. Take him over to your house. Where Breezeblock and the police are waiting for him.'

'TJ's never going to fall for this in a million years.'

'Not at first. But we ring the police again. We tell them we've seen the missing TJ in Helmsdon Wood. And when the squad cars pull up . . .'

'Hmmm.'

'Trust me, Ben,' said Barney, patting my knee patronizingly. 'Now . . . we'd better get down to Reggie's Veggies and ask Belinda if we can borrow some women's clothing.'

'*What?*' I spluttered.

'A disguise, of course. For TJ,' said Barney. 'We'll have to rent the wig.'

'Let me get this straight,' said Belinda. 'You want to borrow a dress, a pair of tights, a bra, some shoes, preferably high-heeled, and a pair of knickers.'

'We can live without the knickers,' said Barney, 'and if the dress was on the baggy side that would be helpful.'

'Radiation-mutated giant bananas I can just about handle, but *this* . . .'

'There is a sane and rational explanation,' said Barney. 'Unfortunately it is extremely secret as of this moment in time. However, I can say that it does involve getting Ben's cousin into the most frightful amount of trouble. And you *did* say that if there was anything you could do to help . . .'

'I trust dry-cleaning is included.'

'That goes without saying.'

'I hope I'm not going to regret this.'

'Scout's honour,' I said.

'OK, then. Tomorrow morning. Here. And make it early. I'm doing the rounds with the van.'

*

We primed Jenks. Then we primed him again. We made him memorize the story and repeat it back to us seven times until he had it off pat.

'And stick to it,' said Barney. 'Don't try to be creative. If Hogmoor gets wind of this one, he might start believing Dr Gravely. And then we will almost certainly end up in the funny farm.'

The following morning, shortly after picking up the clothes from Reggie's Veggies, we were standing with Mum at the desk of the police station, signing in for the day to prove we weren't on the Dover–Calais hovercraft. Barney had just done his signature when he looked up and said to the duty constable, 'Could you give a message to Detective Inspector Hogmoor?'

'OK,' said the constable, licking his pencil and poising it above a Post-It Note. 'Fire away.'

'Tell him TJ's coming back from Sector Seven.' The constable paused and glared at Barney with a look of deep scepticism. 'Quite by chance a wormhole has opened up in the Reality Continuum, creating a new transdimensional portal just above Slough. So we can expect lots of flotsam coming through over the next few days.'

When we'd dumped Mum we headed off to the wig shop.

'The long, blonde one, please,' said Barney, pointing to the top shelf.

The assistant brought the wig down and laid it on the

desk, giving us an I-Don't-Like-Perverts-in-My-Shop look. 'That'll be twelve pounds for the week.'

Barney handed over the money.

'And we'll dry-clean it,' said Jenks, helpfully.

'You do *not* dry-clean wigs,' said the assistant. 'You refrain from getting them dirty in the first place.'

'Take no notice of him,' said Barney. 'Trust me. I'm an expert. Wear wigs all the time. Look at this one.' He tugged his forelock. 'Clean as a whistle.'

Wig on Wheels

'How did you find me, you little snot-rags?' asked TJ, flabbergasted.

'Easy,' I said. 'You were calling from a phone box. I dialled 1471 . . .'

'That's not important right now,' said Barney, darkly.

'Oh, and what *is* important right now, Mr Wise-Guy?' asked TJ.

'Mrs Block.'

'What about the old bag?'

'She's in hospital.'

'On a life support machine,' said Jenks.

'Oh, poor old her,' said TJ sarcastically.

'They found the gun,' said Barney.

'What gun?' asked TJ.

'The air-rifle, you idiot,' said Barney harshly. 'Your dad's.'

'There's only one idiot round here,' replied TJ, 'and it ain't me.'

'They found it at the bottom of the garden,' I said. 'You must have dropped it. Or Fisty must have dropped it. When you were climbing over the fence.'

'Whoa! Now hang on. What *is* all this rubbish?'

'They know,' said Jenks. 'They know about you and him going back to your dad's place. And borrowing the air-rifle. And breaking into Mrs Block's house to get Fisty's ghetto-blaster.'

'What do you mean, "they"?'

'The police, you moron,' said Jenks.

Barney was right. TJ was starting to look flustered.

'Wait a minute, wait a minute,' he said. 'Let's get this straight. You're telling me that Fisty broke into Mrs Block's house with my dad's gun . . .'

'And there was this scuffle,' added Jenks. 'And she got shot. And you . . .'

'Me? Me? Me what? I don't know what the hell you're talking about.'

'You mean you weren't with him?' I asked.

'Course I wasn't with him, you berk,' said TJ.

'Well, *someone* was with him,' said Barney. 'The neighbours saw these two silhouettes running away. And your fingerprints *were* on the gun.'

'Of course my fingerprints are on the gun,' said TJ, beginning to panic.

'Anyway, they've got Fisty banged up at the moment,'

said Jenks. 'And we kind of assumed that he'd ratted on you.'

'Oh . . . God . . . Jeez . . .' TJ put his hands over his face. Then he took his hands away again and sobered up. 'Wait a minute. This is a wind-up, isn't it? I can see it now.' He sneered unpleasantly. 'You little twerps are just trying to scare me, in return for the dartboard stuff, aren't you? Well . . .' He jabbed the side of his head with his finger. 'I'm not stupid. I'm not falling for this one. No way. Besides, even if this were true – which it isn't – why didn't you just ring the police when you found out where I was, eh?'

'TJ,' I said, 'I would *love* to have rung the police. Believe me. So would Dad. So would Mum. But *your* parents, for some incomprehensible reason, are not keen on your being behind bars.'

TJ glowered at me like a cornered beast.

'So Dad's agreed to help you lie low for a bit till everything's calmed down.'

'Look,' said Barney, 'I don't give a monkeys whether you believe us or not. There's a train to Aberdeen tomorrow afternoon at 2.20. We take you to Ben's house. Ben's dad drives you to the station. Your Uncle Bernie meets you at the other end.'

'Just shut it,' said TJ. 'I've listened to enough of this clap-trap.'

Barney looked TJ in the eye. 'Your face has been plastered all over the local news. Ben's parents have been grilled by the police. There's been a squad car parked outside your house for the last seven days . . .'

TJ pursed his lips, his small brain chewing over the information. He was on the edge. He could go either way.

'If you don't believe us, we can go over there and you can see for yourself,' I said, adopting a chummier tone.

TJ did a bit more mental chewing. If he came, it might turn out to be a joke. If he didn't come he'd sit here wondering whether he could ever go home again.

'OK, let's go,' he said, 'but if this *is* a wind-up . . .'

'Relax,' I said.

'Borrow my bike,' said Barney. 'I'll wait here until you get back.'

TJ threw Barney a menacing look. 'How do I know you won't run off with my tent? Or set light to it?'

'Because you'll have my bike.'

'Oh, yeah. Right.'

Jenks and I set off with TJ in tow.

It couldn't have worked out better. Barney timed the call perfectly. The police had just arrived when we pulled up behind the wall on the far side of the road. When TJ saw them the colour actually drained from his face. But the *pièce de résistance* was still to come. One of the constables knocked on the neighbours' door, waited for a woman to open it and said, in a clearly audible voice, 'Good evening, Mrs Buxton. Sorry to disturb you again. You haven't, by any chance, seen the missing Bagnell boy around this evening, have you?'

At this point TJ had to lean down and put his head between his knees and do some very deep breathing.

He was decidedly wobbly on the way back. And when we finally arrived at the copse he was putty in our hands.

'OK. OK,' he said. 'Maybe you're right. Except . . . I mean . . . this is crazy . . . totally crazy. It's nothing to do with me. I never went near that woman's house.'

'So, do you want our help, or not?' asked Barney.

TJ took a deep breath. 'Just get me on that train.' He glared at each of us in turn. 'And no cock-ups, all right. If anything goes wrong, I'll . . .'

'Yeah, yeah, yeah,' replied Barney. 'Listen. We'll be back at one o'clock tomorrow lunchtime. We're going to have to move fast. So get the tent down and your rucksack packed, OK?'

'I'll be ready,' said TJ, trying to sound tough.

'Tomorrow. One o'clock, then,' said Barney, and we turned to go.

We reached the edge of the wood, unlocked our bikes and cycled off down the road. When we were out of shouting distance we skidded to a halt in a farm driveway and lay on our backs in the dust, looking up at the sky, cheering, 'Yes! Yes! Yes!' and came within an inch of being crushed to death by a lorry full of sheep.

The following day I woke up at seven o'clock, unable to sleep any longer, just like on Christmas morning. I ate a hero's breakfast of three Weetabix and two kippers and washed them down with a glass of mango juice to give me vitamin-powered health and energy.

Barney and Jenks arrived at half-nine and we were taken to the police station by Dad for our daily check-in. He remarked, in the car, that we were unnaturally cheerful and Barney said, 'The sky. The flowers. The trees. Who could fail to be happy on a beautiful morning like this, Mr Simpson?'

Dad looked at him and shook his head. 'Just don't tell me about it. Whatever it is. Don't tell me anything. I'm in enough trouble already.'

At the police station, having signed his name, Barney said to the constable at the desk, 'Tell Hogmoor it's today, will you? Stuff has been spewing out of the trans-dimensional corridor all morning. They're handing out helmets in Slough.'

*

'No. No. No. No way. No. That is *ridiculous*. I don't care if the FBI and the CIA and Interpol are looking for me. I am not, repeat *not*, wearing that stuff.'

'Listen, Buster,' said Barney. 'We passed three police cars on the way here. Your face has been on the local news for five nights running. If anyone sees you, you'll be banged up by tea-time. Understand?'

'What was that!?' I muttered nervously.

'What was *what*?' asked TJ.

'I thought I head voices.'

'Go and check it out, Ben,' said Barney, 'while I try and knock some sense into this guy's thick head.'

I slipped away as planned, speeding up when I was out of sight, leaping the fence and rushing across the road to the phone box where I called the police station.

'Good afternoon,' I said, in my best Women's Institute voice. 'I wonder if you can be of assistance.'

'Well, let's see if we can,' said the very pleasant female police officer on the other end of the line.

'I was just driving past Helmsdon Wood on the way to Abthorpe when I was forced to swerve to avoid a naked man running around in the middle of the road.'

'A naked man?'

'In a balaclava.'

'A balaclava?'

'A yellow balaclava.'

'Right.'

'It was quite grotesque.'

'I can imagine . . . Perhaps I should send a couple of officers over there.'

'That would be very kind of you indeed.'

'And you are . . . ?'

'Sheila Jessop. 9 Elms Drive, Abthorpe. And I'm calling from a payphone and I'm afraid my money is about to . . .'

I put the phone down and wiped my fingerprints off the receiver with a handkerchief. I recrossed the road and hid in the bushes at the edge of the wood.

The police arrived in three minutes, parked and got out. I made a rustling noise – the kind of rustling noise a naked man in a balaclava might make if he had seen the police and decided to leap into the nearest undergrowth – waited until the two officers began walking towards the fence, then made my way back to the tent as quickly as I could.

'Police!' I panted; as I burst into the tiny clearing. 'On the road. They're coming into the wood.'

TJ was fuming. 'I don't believe it. It's a set-up. It's just a trick to get me dressed up in this gear, isn't it?'

'TJ,' I pleaded, 'we don't have time to argue about this. Come on! You *have* to believe us.'

TJ and I stared at each other.

A twig crunched. Somewhere to our left a police walkie-talkie squawked briefly into life.

TJ's eyes widened in terror. He looked the way you might look if you'd found a crocodile in your bath. 'OK. OK. OK,' he whispered. 'I'll do it.'

He squirmed out of his clothes and into the dress. Jenks handed TJ's clothes to Barney, who jammed them into the rucksack along with the folded tent. I handed TJ

163

the sock-stuffed bra, the high-heeled shoes and the wig.

The rucksack full, Jenks and Barney headed off towards the bikes while I stayed with TJ, helping him into the stockings and making the final wig-adjustments.

We got out with seconds to spare. Pushing TJ to the ground behind a large log, I turned and saw the two officers emerge into the clearing from between two blackberry bushes.

'What have we got here, then?' said Policeman No. 1, poking at the remains of the fire with the toe of his boot while Policeman No. 2 squatted down and picked up TJ's discarded copy of *VROOM!* magazine.

'That is a tasty piece of Moto Guzzi,' said Policeman No. 23, holding up a double-page spread for Policeman No. 1 to admire.

'The missing Bagnell kid!' said Policeman No. 1, a lightbulb going on over his head.

'What about the missing Bagnell kid?' said Policeman No. 2.

I heard a tiny squeak from TJ and looked down and saw the sweat drip-drip-dripping from underneath his wig.

'Campfire. Motorcycle mags. Deserted wood. Maybe he isn't dead after all,' said Policeman No. 1.

The lightbulb went on over the head of Policeman No. 2.

They looked at one another for a couple of seconds. Then, as one, they turned and ran back to the car to radio the station.

TJ looked up. His face was covered in mud from where

I'd pushed him to the floor. His wig was wonky and his hands were shaking. 'Let's get out of here. Let's get out of here *now*.'

We met up with Jenks and Barney by the bridge.

'Here,' said Jenks to TJ, 'we brought this for you.'

It was his sister's bike. It was pink. It had a women's frame and a white, plastic basket on the front. TJ gritted his teeth and climbed on. We saddled up behind him.

'OK,' said Barney. 'Ben's house.' And we headed off in convoy.

Seventeen Minutes of Unbridled Insanity

It was hard not to laugh, watching TJ cycling just ahead of me, squeezed into a short, floral dress, his too-small stilettos catching on the pedals and his blonde hair flying in the wind as he rode like a madman on the ridiculous pink contraption. But I bit my lip and put my head down.

We reached the end of the cycle track and were about to enter the housing estate when Barney pulled us all up. 'You go ahead, Ben. Check the coast's clear.'

'What do you mean "The coast's clear"?' growled TJ. 'I thought your dad was just going to be waiting and everything.'

'We've had four visits from the police in the last week,' I said. 'If you want to barge through the front door and find Detective Inspector Hogmoor sitting on the sofa grilling Mum then . . .'

'OK,' agreed TJ. 'OK, OK, OK.'

'Relax,' I said. 'It takes ten minutes to drive to the station. We've got loads of time.'

'Go on, Ben,' said Barney. 'We'll wait for you here.'

Two passing boys wolf-whistled TJ. He opened his mouth to shout back at them but Barney grabbed his shoulder. 'Chill out. We don't need you getting into a fight. Not now.'

I cycled off down Mollett Street, past the Kwik Save, then screeched to a halt outside the phone box on the corner of Lewis Avenue. I leapt off my bike and charged inside, pulling the bag of loose change from my pocket.

I rang the police station. 'Hullo, my name's Ben Simpson.'

'Ah yes,' said the policeman on the other end of the line. 'The moron with the fire extinguishers.'

'Er, yeah. Sorry about that. Look . . .'

'What?

'I was just ringing to say that TJ isn't dead. He's turned up at our house.'

The policeman hmmmed for a bit. 'If you don't mind me asking, why aren't your parents ringing up with this information?'

'Because they've got him pinned to the carpet in the lounge.'

'Are you telling the truth, young man?'

'Just tell Detective Inspector Hogmoor to get over here. Now.'

I put the receiver down, crossed my fingers, picked it up again and rang the school.

'Message for Mrs Block,' I said in my best Sheila Jessop voice, 'from Detective Inspector Hogmoor. Tell her to be at the Simpson house in ten minutes.'

'I'm afraid she's in a meeting.'

'Well get her out. This is a matter of life and death.'

I put the phone down and handkerchiefed the receiver. I exited from the phone box, yelled, 'Geronimo!' leapt onto my bike and cycled round the block twelve times to give everyone time to get over to my place ready for the showdown. Then I headed back to the rendezvous point.

'Where the hell have you been?' said TJ, suspiciously.

'Lucky I went on ahead,' I said. 'We could have blown everything.'

'Police?' asked Barney, sagely.

'Swarming,' I replied. 'But it's all right. They've gone now.'

TJ wiped the beads of sweat from his wig-warmed forehead.

'Okey-dokey,' said Barney, 'let's go.'

We cycled into the estate, TJ keeping his head down, trying to see his way through the sheet of blonde hair covering his eyes. Link Road. Flatte Street. Daventry Hill. We were only a hundred yards away now. I crossed my fingers. Breezeblock and the police would be arriving any minute.

'Whoa!' I said. 'Not round the front. We'll go in the back way. Down the alley and up the garden. Play it safe.'

'Good thinking,' agreed TJ.

We turned into the alley, swerved round a man struggling with a wheelbarrow of fertilizer, headed down to the far end and de-biked.

'You wait here,' I said. 'I'll go up first.'

'We'll wait,' said Jenks.

'Thirty seconds,' I said, and slipped through the gate and up the garden.

I opened the kitchen door and stepped inside. The house was worryingly quiet. For a couple of seconds I began to panic, thinking I'd wrecked all of Barney's careful planning with a rubbish Women's Institute impression. Then Dad appeared in the hallway, looking flustered.

'Ben!' he exclaimed. 'What in God's name is going on?'

'Sorry?'

'I went to the door thinking it was the pizza man delivering my Mediterranean Special for lunch. Except it was those two policemen, Pickings and Hogmoor, saying TJ was here. Then the door goes and it's your headmistress saying the police told her to come round. Except Hogmoor and Pickings say they didn't. And your mum, who is just about at her wits' end, is in the lounge trying to calm everyone down.' His face darkened. 'And, Ben, if this has *anything* to do with you . . .'

'Thank goodness,' I said.

Dad stepped towards me, adopting an ominous son-strangling posture. 'This *has* got something to do with you, hasn't it?'

'Yeah,' I said. 'But it's all right. We found TJ. We've

got him with us. He's in the garden.'

Dad looked stunned.

'Just keep them in the lounge,' I pleaded. 'Keep them talking for two minutes. That's all. This is important. Please, Dad.'

'I want an explanation.'

'Later. Honestly.'

Dad shook his head in exasperation. 'Sometimes I think I must have done something really, really terrible in a past life to deserve all this . . .'

'Please?'

'You have two minutes, Ben. That's all. I mean it. Any longer and I am going to personally hand you over to your headmistress and those two policemen, OK?'

'And keep the lounge door shut.'

I waited for Dad to leave the kitchen. Then I leant out of the back door and signalled to Barney, Jenks and TJ. They trotted up the garden. TJ had torn his tights in at least three places, his wig was skew-whiff and he was holding a stiletto in each hand. For a fraction of a second, I actually felt sorry for him.

Then I remembered the hot chocolates and the errands and the money missing from my Darth Vader bank and the grilling from Mrs Block and being suspended from school and being under suspicion for murder; and I didn't feel sorry for him any longer.

Barney, Jenks and TJ tiptoed into the kitchen.

'Dad's getting the car out,' I explained. 'TJ, go into the lounge. Quietly. Look out of the front window. Dad will give you the signal.'

TJ took a deep breath and gave me a thumbs-up.

'Half an hour,' I said, 'and you'll be on that train.'

'Right,' he said. 'Right.'

He turned and crept gingerly up the hallway. Out of the corner of my eye I saw Barney opening his bag and beginning to retrieve the camcorder. 'Couldn't resist,' he whispered. 'Got to record this one for posterity.'

TJ gripped the handle of the lounge door, paused briefly, turned it and stepped inside.

Barney turned to Jenks. 'Get the bikes. If we're lucky we may have a chase on our hands. And I want to get as much of it down on tape as possible.'

'Sure thing,' said Jenks, running out of the kitchen.

I found out later, from Dad, what happened during the first few minutes of unbridled insanity.

TJ came into the room, shut the door and leant his back against it. His eyes were closed and he was breathing deeply.

He didn't keep his eyes closed for long, however, because Mum said, rather sharply, 'Who on earth are you?'

TJ opened his eyes and said something like, 'GAKKK!'

'This is outrageous!' complained Mrs Block. 'I am not going to stand here and . . .'

TJ span round and saw the awesome figure of the angry headmistress and exclaimed, 'You're meant to be on a life support machine!'

'WHAT!!??' roared Mrs Block.

'TJ!' exclaimed Mum. 'What are you doing in that ridiculous get-up?'

171

'The Bagnell boy,' said Detective Inspector Hogmoor, and the two policemen lunged.

A lot of furniture was overturned in the short, hectic chase which followed, as Pickings and Hogmoor tried to get hold of TJ and TJ dodged and weaved, hurling stilettos at them and shouting, 'It wasn't me! It wasn't me! I didn't do it! I didn't shoot her!' forgetting that the supposedly bullet-peppered headmistress was standing only a few metres away, trying very hard not to get sucked into the fray.

Somehow, TJ got back to the door before the policemen did and plunged into the corridor. Weirdly, as he did this, the front doorbell rang. TJ yanked it open.

'One Mediterranean Special,' said a man in a motor-cycle helmet and a luminous, orange safety-vest with the words PIZZA HEAVEN printed on it.

TJ shoved him to the ground, spraying the inside of the porch with pre-cut sections of Mediterranean Special, ran out into the drive, leapt onto the PIZZA HEAVEN moped and hit the ignition.

The pizza delivery man sat up briefly and was then knocked to the ground for a second time as two policemen, Mum, Dad, Mrs Block, me, Barney, Jenks and three bicycles stormed through the cloud of descending anchovies and tomatoes and feta cheese and trampled him back into the mat.

TJ put the moped into gear, twisted the throttle and did a neat little turn, spraying the approaching policemen with gravel and exiting smartly from the drive.

'Lights! Camera! Action!' shouted Barney as the three

of us leapt onto our bikes and careered through the front gate after him, Barney wobbling a little on account of the camcorder at his shoulder.

The gravel-sprayed policemen leapt into their car and Dad, infected by the excitement, leapt into ours, dragging a protesting Mum with him.

At the end of the road, TJ realized that his hopes of out-pacing a police car on a PIZZA HEAVEN moped were pretty slim and that he stood a considerably better chance of evading capture on the rough terrain of the park. Unfortunately the park was at the other end of the road, so he slammed on the brakes and swung the moped through 180 degrees.

The police car swerved up onto the pavement to avoid him and Dad swerved onto the opposite pavement to avoid the police car, noisily removing a small piece of rear-bumper in the process. TJ squeezed the throttle and drove straight through the middle of the following crowd, scattering us in all directions and knocking the pizza delivery man to the ground for a third time as he stumbled out into the road wondering where his vehicle had got to.

The tyres of the police car shrieked as Pickings hurled it into reverse and started the siren. We span round and headed off back up the road.

TJ swerved through the park gate and onto the grass, closely followed by Barney, Jenks and me at the head of the chasing pack. Over our shoulders we could hear more tyre-shrieks and the slamming of several car doors as Hogmoor, Pickings, Mum and Dad got out to give chase on foot.

173

'Look!' yelled Jenks.

We looked. In the middle of the park stood Fisty Morgan, staring in our direction, wondering what on earth was going on and why this muscular woman in a blonde wig was pulling up next to him on a moped.

What TJ and Fisty said to each other we never found out, though Barney did manage to record the brief and violent encounter on video.

Clearly TJ still thought Fisty had framed him. Despite Mrs Block being very much not on a life support machine. Despite Fisty himself being very much not in police custody. So he rocked forward and nutted Fisty on the forehead. Fisty's skull, however, was pretty thick, so the nutting had very little effect. He grabbed at TJ's dress. TJ hit the gas, leaving the top half of the dress in Fisty's hand and sped towards the far side of the park wearing a wig, a short floral skirt and a sock-filled brassiere.

Fisty joined in the chase.

We nearly caught TJ at the edge of the park when a crowd of very small schoolchildren came in through the gates, shepherded by a couple of teachers, forcing TJ to slow down and execute a tricky slalom through the scrum.

The two policemen, who obviously did cross-country running in their spare time, were now close behind us. Dad was behind them. And Mum was in close pursuit, running neck-and-neck with the pizza delivery man. Mrs Block had probably gone home by this time for a stiff gin and a hot bath.

'Faster!' shouted Jenks.

But we couldn't go any faster. And TJ had the advantage now. He was on the tarmac of the High Street. And he might have got away were it not for a really quite extraordinary coincidence.

Dad had been wondering, over the past few days, why Trish had given up phoning. The reason, we soon found out, was the lack of a ship-to-shore phone facility on the whaling vessel which had recently docked at Talula to transport the hotel's residents to a small airfield in the Pitcairn Islands.

Arriving at Heathrow after eighteen hours in the air, Trish's first thought was to go home and shower off the smell of whale-blubber. Harry, however, decided that it would be better if they went and picked up their miscreant son. Trish reluctantly agreed.

They had almost reached our house when Harry was startled by the appearance of a crazed young man in a wig, bra and floral dress overtaking an oncoming milk float at high speed and leaving him absolutely no room to manoeuvre. Harry hauled on the steering wheel to avoid a fatal collision and attempted to park inside a lamppost which turned out to be far more solid than the bonnet of his Ford Probe.

TJ was equally startled by the appearance of a fast-moving Ford Probe being driven by someone looking like his father and taking up almost all of the road. He swerved, skidded and rapidly reached the limit of his moped-control skills. The front tyre hit the kerb and reared up. He wheelied across the pavement, sliced an elderly lady's tartan shopping trolley into two separate sections, hit a waste bin, went over the handlebars and sailed through the plate-glass window of Reggie's Veggies.

Harry was the first to arrive on the scene, sporting a large, blood-stained dent in his forehead where he had head-butted the steering wheel. It was therefore quite lucky for TJ that he was wearing the wig, bra and skirt combination because if Harry had recognized his son before the police arrived he might very well have killed him.

'You crazy, pea-brained dolt!' yelled Harry, wading through the scree of shattered glass and crushed avocados. 'You have just caused six thousand quid's worth of damage, do you realize that?'

TJ scraped the squashed fruit from his face. 'Dad!' he yelped.

At this point Harry went into some kind of weird seizure, having just realized a) that the crazy, peabrained dolt was his son, b) that his son was a homicidal maniac, and c) that he had also become a transvestite.

'Hey! That's my dress!' screamed Belinda, appearing from behind the barricade of toppled shelves.

'Oooh! Belinda! Help! My back's gone again!' shouted Reggie from somewhere invisible.

Hogmoor and Pickings appeared, panting, just behind us.

Jenks turned to Hogmoor. 'See. We didn't kill TJ after all.'

'Come here, you little moron!' yelled Harry, reemerging from his seizure and striding forward into the fruit-swamp. 'I'll get you . . . !'

'Not if I get there first,' shouted Fisty, barging his way between the two policemen, jumping into the shop window and diving towards the half-buried TJ.

'Easy! Easy!' shouted Sergeant Pickings, jumping forward in a vain attempt to separate the three of them.

'Ben!' shouted Dad, staggering to a halt. 'What on earth . . . ?' But he was too out of breath to talk.

Fisty punched TJ. TJ punched Fisty. Harry heaved Fisty out of the way and punched TJ himself. Fisty punched Harry. Sergeant Pickings fought his way between them, shouting, 'Whoa! Whoa!' And Fisty punched Sergeant Pickings.

Behind me I heard a plaintive, little voice saying, sadly,

in an Italian accent, 'My moped! Look what he's a-done to my moped!'

Detective Inspector Hogmoor lowered his face into his hands and said, 'That's it. I've had enough. A little cottage in the country. That's all I want. Bit of gardening. Game of golf every weekend. Cricket on the telly.' I turned and looked at him. There was a crushed anchovy stuck to the bald spot in the middle of his head. He looked as if he might be crying.

Barney stepped through the shop window and stood over TJ, Fisty, Harry and Sergeant Pickings with the camcorder running until they finally stopped punching each other.

'Super, everybody,' he said. 'That was lovely. Right. I think we can call that a rap.'

Back to Turtle-Waxing the Nissan Micra

So everyone lived happily ever after.

Well, *we* did anyway.

Harry and TJ were driven away by the police, though whether Harry was there as the Responsible Adult or whether they were planning to charge him with Disorderly Conduct on his own account, I never found out. Fisty was very sensibly driven away in a separate police car.

When we finally headed back home to scrape the Mediterranean Special off the inside of the porch and put the furniture back in place, Barney, Jenks and I assumed we were in for some stiff questioning from Trish. But she seemed more concerned with getting that hot shower. She stayed long enough to put one set of clothes through the washer-dryer then rang for a taxi and left without a word. We haven't seen or heard from the family since.

A result, I think.

Mum, however, was less easily satisfied.

We explained how we'd tracked TJ down. How he'd gone mad. How he'd started wearing women's clothes. How we'd tried to hand him into the police. How he'd tried to escape . . .

Mum knew there was more to it than this but we weren't telling. And since we've not spoken to the Bagnells since, she's never found out.

Dad knew the truth, of course. But he wasn't telling either. He'd been in enough trouble over the past few weeks. Plus, he owed us. We'd provided him with more entertainment in twenty minutes than he'd had all year.

'Better than Turtle-Waxing the Nissan Micra and buying hardy perennials at the garden centre, wasn't it?' I said.

'I don't think I've laughed so much since . . . well, since the Atomic Vaporizer went off.'

'And what, precisely, was the "Atomic Vaporizer"?' asked Mum, looking suspicious.

'Got any of that delicious coffee cake left, Mrs Simpson?' asked Barney, diplomatically

Belinda wasn't too chuffed either.

There was only half the dress left, so the offer of dry-cleaning was kind of beside the point. The tights were ripped, the bra had been stretched to triple D and we wouldn't find the second stiletto – lodged behind the

180

curtain rail in the lounge – until Mum did her annual spring-clean nine months later.

So we apologized and grovelled and pooled all our pocket money. I sold Dr Scream's House of Horror for a worryingly large wad of cash to a kid in the third form. Then Mum and I went down to the Grosvenor Centre and she helped me buy a selection of replacement clothing. Mum being a good bargain hunter, we had some spare cash left over at the end, and we were passing the jeweller's on the way home when something caught my eye.

Back at home I wrapped everything in stripy gold paper and delivered it to Reggie's Veggies while Belinda was out with the van.

We were all so excited by the weekend's events that we totally forgot about going back to school on Monday morning and didn't remember until Breezeblock rang Mum just after lunch and demanded to know where we were. Mum, who'd had quite enough of being patronized by the old witch, pointed out that she'd banned us.

'Mrs Simpson,' said Mrs Block, 'I would have thought it was perfectly obvious that they are no longer banned now the Bagnell boy has been found.'

'Apologize,' said Mum.

'*Apologize!?*' exploded Mrs Block.

'Apologize and I'll send Ben back to school,' replied Mum.

'What for, might I ask?'

'For treating my family like criminals,' said Mum. 'For

calling my husband insane. For refusing to believe any of us. For assuming my son could have done any harm to a boy who is, and always has been, quite obviously barking mad and who had quite clearly run away.'

There was a silence on the other end of the phone for some considerable time. Then a little voice said, 'Mrs Simpson . . . I'm sorry.'

'Do it properly,' said Mum, 'in writing,' and put the phone down.

On Tuesday morning we reclaimed the tape of *The Invasion of the Killer Bananas* and the Atomic Vaporizer from the police station and returned the wig.

The woman in the shop was not pleased when she looked into the damp Sainsbury's bag which Jenks had dumped on the counter. Gingerly, she upended it and the moist, clotted wig slid out like a drowned dog.

'What is this?' she asked, pointing at the matted hair.

Barney stepped closer and examined it. 'That one in particular is kiwi-fruit, I think. But it is rather difficult to tell. They tend to go the same kind of brown after a day or two.'

The assistant pulled back her shoulders and said, 'I am charging you £65 for having destroyed this item.'

'Run!' said Jenks.

We ran.

On Thursday evening, Barney and Jenks came round to my place for waffles and Tizer 'n' pineapple cocktails and the first showing of *Moped of Fire (certificate U).*

'No mixing. No editing. No animation. And absolutely no bananas,' he said, 'except a few squashed ones in the final scene. Just straightforward, no-nonsense, on-the-spot, documentary reporting.'

'Sounds good,' I said.

Barney patted me on the shoulder. 'Ben . . . It is su-*perb.*'

Mum, Dad, Barney, Jenks and I had just dimmed the lights and settled down with our waffles when the door-bell rang. Dad got up and wandered into the hall. A couple of seconds later he reappeared with Belinda.

'This is a nice surprise,' said Mum.

'*Gnnngk,*' said Barney, through a mouthful of waffle.

'Ben,' she said, 'Barney, Jenks . . . I just wanted to say sorry for shouting at you the other day. And thanks for the clothes. They're great. Better than the lot I gave you, actually, so one of you has excellent taste.' Mum winked at me. 'And thanks, too, for these.' She pulled her hair back to reveal the two tiny Z-shaped ear-studs. 'Strange. But nice. Thanks.'

Barney looked at me and said, 'Ben . . . you are *such* an outrageous smoothie.' My face went crimson. He turned to Belinda. 'Not in a hurry, are you?'

'No, not really. Why?'

'Sit down and grab yourself a waffle. We've got something which I think you might enjoy.'

'Well, if you insist,' said Belinda. She walked round the sofa and plonked herself down next to me. Mum handed her a waffle-stacked side-plate.

'Lights, please, Jenks,' said Barney.

Jenks dimmed the lights.

Barney turned the TV volume up and hit PLAY.

AGENT Z AND THE PENGUIN FROM MARS

by Mark Haddon

*Jenks was squirming back out of the hole with a
wriggly penguin in his arms when I heard the sound
of heavy keeper-boots running towards us.
'Holy Moses!' I hissed and turned to look for
Barney. But Barney had vanished.*

Dennis Sidebottom has moved next door to Ben –
bringing his squeaky-clean kids with him. The
Crane Grove Crew – Ben, Barney and Jenks –
soon find themselves on the Sidebottom blacklist.
Accused of being troublemakers and a bad
influence, they decide to shake up the Sidebottom
universe with the help of Agent Z, a meteorite
and a stolen penguin.

It's Agent Z's finest hour!

'A series of climaxes which get funnier and
funnier . . .' *Books for Keeps*

0 09 971291 1

RED FOX

THE CURIOUS INCIDENT OF THE DOG IN THE NIGHT-TIME

by Mark Haddon

Fifteen-year-old Christopher has Asperger's Syndrome, a form of autism. He has a photographic memory. He understands maths. He understands science. What he can't understand are other human beings.

When he finds his neighbour's dog, Wellington, lying dead on a neighbour's lawn, he decides to track down the killer and write a murder mystery novel about it. In doing so, however, he uncovers other mysteries that threaten to bring his whole world crashing down around him.

The Curious Incident of the Dog in the Night-Time is an astonishing novel– funny, sad and utterly unputdownable.

0 09 945676 1

DEFINITIONS

David Fickling Books
OXFORD · NEW YORK